CU00683577

# Christmas at Winterbourne
## (A Memoir in the Making)

## Jen Silver

# Christmas at Winterbourne
## (A Memoir in the Making)

Jen Silver

Affinity
eBook Press
NZ
2016

Christmas at Winterbourne
(A Memoir in the Making)
© 2016 by Jen Silver

Affinity E-Book Press NZ LTD
Canterbury, New Zealand

1st Edition

ISBN: 978-0-947528-06-5

All rights reserved.

No part of this book may be reproduced in any form without the express permission of the author and publisher. Please note that piracy of copyrighted materials violate the author's rights and is Illegal.

This is a work of fiction. Names, character, places, and incidents are the product of the author's imagination or are used fictitiously and any resemblance to actual persons living or dead, businesses, companies, events, or locales is entirely coincidental

Editor: Angela Koenig
Proof Editor: Alexis Smith
Cover Design: Irish Dragon Designs

# Acknowledgments

This book has been a long time in the making. I started writing the original story twenty-five years ago. The character, Kim Russell, has stayed with me a long time and I'm thrilled she has finally been given her coming out party, so to speak.

Thankful, as always, to the team at Affinity: Julie, Mel and Nancy. Also to Irish Dragon Designs for a cover I feel conveys a sense of the place in the story. Mary H offered perceptive comments in her beta editing role and Angela did another very thorough job on the final editing stage.

Thanks to my wife, Anne, whose continued love and support gives me the time and space to write the stories that come into my head.

I would also like to acknowledge the encouragement I've received from readers of my other books—all helping to give me the confidence to keep on writing.

The dedication is for my sister, Sally—with apologies for taking her name in vain by giving it to one of the characters who bears no resemblance to her whatsoever. But she is responsible for providing the tale of a misguided attempt to smuggle Christmas crackers into Amsterdam.

# Dedication

For Sally

# Table of Contents

# Also by Jen Silver

The Circle Dance

### Starling Hill Trilogy
Starting Over
Arc Over Time
Carved in Stone

### Short Stories
There Was a Time
The Christmas Sweepstake (Affinity's 2014 Christmas Collection)
Beltane in Space (It's In Her Kiss – Affinity Charity Anthology)

# Chapter One

## Arrivals

Wil gazed out over the valley. This time of year, two days before Christmas, the landscape offered the tall, imposing outlines of bare oak and chestnut trees, interspersed with spots of greenery, the holly and the ivy. Wil had time for another canter through the trails before heading back to the house, a house full of chaos. She had been hoping for a quiet family Christmas, just herself and Gaby, but Gaby was expecting their first child and wanted her mother there. So it was the in-laws plus a few more houseguests. Gaby's parents would be fine. Her mum would help with the cooking and her dad liked pottering around the stables. It was the other booked-in guests who might be a problem.

Winterbourne House was a popular lesbian retreat, deep in the Sussex countryside. Wil had inherited it from her adopted mother, Kim Russell. Not that Kim would have thought of herself as a mother, but the reclusive author was the closest thing to a parent she had experienced. Wil and Gaby had renovated and modernised the old country house and started taking guests in 2000. Felicity Evans and her partner, Rose, ran the stables. Both now in their late seventies, they didn't show any sign of slowing down. In fact, Rose was dropping hints about getting married.

The final gallop was followed by a leisurely cool-down trot and walk for the last mile. Upon reaching the stables, Wil slipped off Paddy and led her back to her stall. The silver mare stood quietly for a quick rub down and accepted Wil's offering of an apple gracefully before turning her attention to the fresh bundle of hay.

Felicity met Wil at the door of the tack room.

"Gaby wants you back at the house." Felicity didn't waste words with conversational pleasantries at the best of times.

"You can take care of these, then." Wil shoved the saddle and bridle into her waiting arms and set off at a sprint for the half-mile journey up to the house. Gaby could normally take any situation in her stride but this pregnancy was taking its toll, leaving her exhausted in the evenings. She was putting it down to her age. However, Wil thought it was more likely because she wouldn't relinquish any of her work. Gaby oversaw everything to do with the business from the accounting to the cooking.

"Can you do a pick up from the station?" Gaby threw the words over her shoulder as soon as Wil arrived in the kitchen.

"Sure, babe." Wil leaned in for a kiss but Gaby turned her head aside so Wil's lips only brushed a few wisps of black hair. She sighed. "Who is it I'm meeting?"

"That couple from Manchester who booked last week and someone else. I didn't catch the name." After fifteen years of living in the country, Gaby's English was nearly perfect, but sometimes she would deliberately pretend she didn't understand. Today looked like one of those days.

"Okay. Do I have time to get changed?" Wil looked down at her attire. She was wearing mud-spattered jodhpurs and riding boots.

"No. And you're fine. They'll expect you to look like that. Now, go. I need to finish these pies." With her almost-full-term extended stomach Gaby could barely reach the counter to roll out the pastry.

Dismissed, Wil walked back down the stone-flagged passage to the front hall. She ducked into the downstairs loo. Time at least to have a pee and wash her hands before driving to the train station to meet the new arrivals. Their friends from London were arriving later in the day, and three other guests were making their own way to the house.

Ten minutes later Wil was on the platform watching the train slowly chugging up the track. She thought this connection with the wider world might stop running soon with so few travellers using it. Three carriages and only three passengers alighted. Two she didn't know, probably the Mancunians. The other, a tall blonde woman, looked vaguely familiar and made a beeline for her.

"Wil!"

As the taller woman wrapped her in a bone-crushing embrace, the realisation hit. "Clare?"

She pulled back and gave Wil a dazzling smile. "Surprise! And you haven't changed a bit."

Wil smiled back. "Yeah. Neither have you. Why didn't you let me know you were coming?"

"Bit of a last minute decision. I'll tell you later."

"Excuse me. Are you Wil Tyler?" The interruption came from one of the other women waiting as the train moved off noisily.

"Yes. Sorry. The car's this way." Wil picked up Clare's case and headed to the car. She was barely concentrating as she drove back, aware of Clare sitting beside her. The two in the back had introduced themselves as JJ and Shelley. Even if there had been a dozen passengers to choose from at the station, she could have picked them out. They had "dyke" written all over them and they weren't dressed for the country. JJ was even wearing leather trousers.

Wil turned the car into the drive and continued at a slow pace past the Lodge by the entrance. The two dogs usually stayed near the stables but she didn't want to jolt her passengers with a sudden stop if they ran out in front of the car.

"Is it far to the house?" one of the women in the back seat asked.

"About half a mile."

Wil could see from her face as she glanced into the rearview mirror that this answer didn't please her. However, the one called JJ, seemed to be taking in her surroundings with delight and made her pleasure known as Wil parked up in front of the house.

"Wow. It actually looks like it does on the website. Hope we get some snow."

"We don't get much in the way of snow around here, but we may get lucky this year."

"You've done a great job, kiddo." Clare squeezed her knee.

Wil opened the boot to get the cases out. She wanted to get the couple settled in so she could talk to Clare. It had been fifteen years since she had last seen her. And neither of them had been in a good space then. Too soon after Kim's untimely death.

Wil showed JJ and Shelley to their room. It was the second largest one in the house and had once been her own bedroom. Gaby's parents were staying in the bigger *en suite* next to it. Clare was going to have to make do with one of the smaller rooms, but it also had its own bathroom. Leaving her there to unpack, Wil suggested they meet downstairs in the study when Clare was ready.

Carrying on up another flight of stairs to the top floor she entered the domain she shared with Gaby, a private living space away from the guest areas. There was plenty of room with two double *en-suite* bedrooms plus their own sitting room and kitchenette. Wil had spent the last few months turning the storage area, which had been a nursery once before, into a bedroom for the new arrival. The sofa was a recent addition, ostensibly for Gaby to relax on while breast-feeding, but Wil suspected it was she who would be sleeping on it once the baby arrived.

She had a quick shower and changed into jeans and a sweatshirt, throwing her muddy riding gear into the laundry basket. Clare Finlayson. She couldn't believe it. The Australian actress had disappeared off the radar for all these years and now here she was, at Winterbourne again.

Wil went in search of Gaby to let her know the identity of the mystery guest but she wasn't in the kitchen. An enticing aroma of mince pies assaulted Wil's nostrils. For an Italian, Gaby had quickly, and extremely competently, adapted to English cooking. Her roast dinners, complete with Yorkshire puddings were second to none. Even with the prospect of a full house for Christmas lunch, Gaby was determined to produce the meal herself, and dismissed the small matter of possibly giving birth at the same time.

Wil went into the study and placed another log on the fire. It had just taken nicely, sending flames up the chimney, when Clare arrived.

"You really have done wonders with this place," she enthused as Wil put a glass of red wine in her hand.

"Well, it's been hard work at times. And anyway, Gaby's really the driving force. Without her, I think I would have given up a long time ago."

"Where is she? The wonder woman?"

"Probably giving the local butcher a hard time about the delivery of the turkeys. So, what brings you here after all this time?"

"Work, actually." Clare sipped at her wine.

Wil remembered the first time they had met, in this very room. The actress had been in Hong Kong filming a martial arts movie when she heard about Kim's death. She arrived at Winterbourne several weeks too late for the funeral. Wil had found it strange to meet the woman who had been Kim's lover. It wasn't the best of times for either of them.

"A TV series," Clare added. "I thought they just wanted me to be a consultant, but when I talked to them last week, they asked me to be in it. Flattering at my age. Still, I'm not sure I want to play Shay again. I said I would think about it."

Wil closed her eyes and took a large gulp from her own glass. The television company had also contacted her, as she held the rights to Kim's novels. Kim's legacy, as well as the house, was a series of books about a lesbian detective, Amy Ransom, based in Sydney. All ten books had been made into movies. Clare had starred in numbers four and seven as the baddie, Shay Finch.

"You know," Wil said, eyes still closed, "I really thought we'd seen the last of Amy when number ten was filmed."

"It's the way it is these days. Rather than think up a new storyline, they just re-make something that had a popular following. And lesbians are in now. Look at the success of *Orange is the New Black*. There's even talk of bringing back *The L Word*."

"And making *Star Wars VII* with the original cast who are now thirty-five years older. I mean, really. Set in an old folks home in a galaxy far, far away! At least Blake's out of it."

Clare nodded. "I'm glad I wasn't there."

Gemma Blake, the Canadian actress who played Amy Ransom in all ten movies, had suffered a near-fatal accident during the filming of number ten. She had always insisted on doing her own stunts and this one had gone wrong.

"Do you still keep in touch?"

"No. It's not something I'm proud of, but I don't think I could bear to see her as she is now. Although I've heard on the grapevine that she's getting some feeling back in her legs and may be able to walk again, at least with the aid of a mechanical walker."

They both stared into the fire, flames licking around the log, each with their memories.

"Wil! I thought you checked all the guest rooms." Gaby burst in, her long black hair falling loosely around her shoulders. "Mama found this in the closet." The large, rainbow-coloured dildo landed with a thud on the couch between Clare and Wil.

"Oh, shit. Sorry. I'm sure I looked in there."

"Well, you'd think someone would have missed that," Clare drawled.

Wil watched as her partner processed who this stranger was, seated comfortably in the study. The room was off limits to the paying guests.

"I'm sorry," Gaby said finally. "I'm sure I should know you."

Clare stood up; the tall actress towered over Gaby. "We met once, a long time ago. Clare Finlayson."

"Oh, yes." She nodded, but Wil thought she was only being polite. She didn't look like she remembered Clare at all. She turned to Wil again. "The Canadians have arrived, so there's only the one guest from London still to come. Mark will be here in a few minutes with the drinks order. Do you think you could help him bring in the boxes?"

"Sure. No problem." Wil picked up the dildo and waved it around. "Apart from finding this, are your parents happy with their room?"

"Yes, of course. Why wouldn't they be?" Gaby turned away abruptly and left.

Wil stroked the dildo absent-mindedly. "She's been like this for a few weeks. I don't know what I've done to upset her."

"Well, she looks like she's gonna drop the baby any day now. Is this your first?"

"Yes."

"So she's probably a bit nervous about it."

"Not likely. Gaby has nerves of steel."

They both stared into the fire. It was Clare who broke the silence with a change of subject.

"Sounds like you have a full house for the festivities. Who else is here?"

"Yeah, it's going to be busy. The two I picked up with you from the station are from Manchester. Then there's the Canadian couple who have just arrived, Candice and Marguerite. As far as the other actual paying guests go, there's just yourself and another single, Sally from London. Gaby's parents arrived yesterday. Christmas Day we'll also have Mark and Toby here from the pub in the village. Oh, and Ade and Rita are coming down later this evening. I think you met them before."

"How could I forget? Ade brought me here that time and she drives like a maniac."

Wil laughed. "She's settled down a bit now. Anyway, I better go and help Mark. We've got a few crates of champagne to shift. You might want to go into the guest lounge and see if anyone else has arrived. It'll be mince pies and sherry shortly."

"Great. I don't want to miss out on any of these quaint British traditions."

Wil left Clare to make her own way into the other room and deposited the dildo in the Lost and Found box in the cupboard under the stairs. *Don't know which charity will be getting this if it goes unclaimed.* Maybe after the baby was born, she could interest Gaby in experimenting with it. Shaking that erotically charged image out of her head, Wil continued down the passageway to find Mark.

†

"Will you look at this, hon?" JJ stood at the window of their bedroom. The view encompassed a wide expanse of perfectly manicured lawn with a light breeze ruffling the bare branches of the trees on the edge of the woods. Near the entrance to the path leading into the woodland there was something that looked like a wire frame sculpture of two horses eating grass. She would have to go out and take a closer look.

"What is it?" Shelley was unpacking their case and hanging things in the closet, noisily.

It had only taken JJ a few moments to remove the few items of clothing she'd brought, leaving Shelley to deal with her larger wardrobe selection.

"Looks like a great place for walking. Wouldn't it be fun if it snowed?"

"Oh yeah. And then we'd be stuck here with a bunch of weirdos like in some Agatha Christie novel."

JJ turned around and watched as Shelley put her underwear in the top drawer of the dresser.

"I thought this is what you wanted. Somewhere quiet, away from the usual Christmas clatter. A nice country house retreat, and a lesbian one at that." It had been a long, tiring journey. On reaching London's King's Cross station, they'd taken the tube to Waterloo, a train to Brighton and then the small local train to this out-of-the-way location in deepest Sussex. She was enchanted by the whole place as soon as they arrived, but Shelley looked like she was getting into a mood.

Shelley zipped the suitcase shut and slipped it in behind the easy chair next to the dresser. Even when they were on holiday, everything had to have its place.

JJ picked up the programme that had been left on the bed. "Look, there's sherry and mince pies in the lounge now. Let's go down and you can check out for yourself just how weird the other guests might be."

"I don't know why I thought this would be a good idea. There isn't even a decent Wi-Fi signal." Shelley poked at her phone.

"So what. They advertise the place as a retreat. Getting away from the distractions of everyday life. That's the whole idea. Look, there's an indoor pool here, lots of places to walk without going near a road. It's perfect. Come on, Shel. Don't spoil it."

Shelley sat down in the chair. "I don't even like sherry."

"Well, I'll drink yours and you can hold out for the champagne. Come on. Smile. Time to get into the Christmas spirit."

†

Sally stopped at the end of the lane to survey the lie of the land. It was exactly as she had imagined, visually aided by Google Maps, but this is where the computer images had ended. The Lodge stood solidly by the entrance to the property and she could hear the sounds of horses from the stables she knew were located a short distance away.

She continued her journey up the drive that led to the house. The deciduous trees had lost their leaves, but the woodland on either side still looked enticing with enough greenery to make for an enjoyable walk. Holly bushes, rowans with bright red berries, towering conifers; with a bit of snow it would be a winter wonderland.

The walk from the train station was four-point-three miles according to the map. And it was an additional point-five mile up the long driveway. She could have contacted the owner of Winterbourne House for a lift, as stated in the

Christmas programme instructions, but she had wanted to walk, to get a feel for the place and absorb the atmosphere.

When the house finally came into view, she stopped again and reached for her phone. Some photos would be useful. Sally took a few quick snaps before walking up to the front door, which was also worthy of being photographed. It wouldn't have looked out of place in a gothic horror film—solid wood bolstered by black metal studs. She unhooked her bulky backpack and pressed the more modern-looking bell push on the frame.

The woman who opened the door had to be Wil Tyler. Short, the body weight of an underfed gnat, and cropped red hair. Sally smiled at her and got a cheerful host-type smile in return. A smile that almost reached the younger woman's eyes, but not quite.

"You must be Sally Hunter. Please come in."

Sally entered the hallway and took in the wood panelling and wide staircase. All very country house and pretty much what she'd expected. The impressive fir tree reached all the way up to the high ceiling of the entrance hall. She could just see the golden star topping it off. It was tastefully decorated with red and silver glass ornaments.

"Is that a Norwegian pine?" she asked.

"No. We grow our own. It's a Sussex spruce." Wil led the way towards the foot of the stairs. She pointed to the large oak-paneled door on the left. "The lounge is through there. Mince pies and sherry are available from now until it's time for the pre-dinner champagne and canapés. I'll show you up to your room. Just come down when you're ready."

"Thank you." Sally resettled her backpack across her shoulders and followed Wil up the stairs. She revised her opinion of her host's body: a well-shaped butt in tight-fitting jeans. She gave herself a mental slap. She wasn't here to lust after anyone; it was work, purely research. But if there were distractions like this, it was going to be difficult to keep her mind on the job. *You've come to a lesbian retreat, what the hell did you expect?* She reminded herself why she was single and not in the market. Still not fully recovered from the fall-out from her last relationship, she wasn't going to even think about getting involved again for a very long time.

The room was well appointed, with a queen-size bed, fully kitted-out *en-suite* bathroom, and two views. One large window overlooked a well-kept lawn with trees beyond, and a smaller side window showed the drive she had walked up. She knew that the property extended through many acres of woodland with bridleways and paths leading eventually to the creek, the winter bourne of the house's name, a seasonal waterway, dry as a bone in summer. She did find that hard to believe with some of the wet summers they'd had recently.

Three framed photographs on the walls were artistically shot images of the landscape. One of them, when she examined it closely, showed a ghostly image of a grey horse grazing in the foreground. There was, no doubt, a story attached to that. And it was a story she was looking for.

She dumped her rucksack on the chair and pulled out her clothes, a crease-free sparkly top and black slacks that would do for the evening ahead. A quick shower and change into her fresh garments and she was good to go. Her short blonde hair only needed a quick brush. It would dry naturally and she was sure the lounge would contain a large fireplace with tree-trunk-sized logs burning away.

†

Clare stared into the fire, flames leaping up the chimney with gusto. She wasn't sure why she had come. Curious, perhaps, to see what Wil and Gaby had done with the place. They had only been kids when she first met them, barely in their twenties, not that much younger but she had felt older. Wil still had the baby dyke look about her although she must be heading for forty now. With her impish grin and that short red hair, she was still cute. And Gaby, well, she had been a stunner, and had also hardly aged. Pregnancy brought out her lustrous eyes, and her long black hair had lost none of its shine.

They had done an amazing job with the house. The website also showed a swimming pool located in a separate, chalet-style building in the grounds, complete with sauna and Jacuzzi. Other activities, along with horse riding, included cycling, and walking or jogging the numerous trails through the woods.

Clare glanced at the sideboard. A tray containing the tiny bite-size mince pies and sherry glasses looked inviting. There were three bottles, dry, medium, and sweet, she guessed. Something for all tastes. Helping herself to a dry sherry, she popped a pie into her mouth and settled down in one of the comfortable seats by the fire.

Magazines littered the tabletop. Along with *Horse and Hounds*, she spotted *Diva* and *Curve*. Well, maybe she should just relax and not question her motives for visiting too closely.

Deep into a film review in the American magazine, she didn't notice the newcomers until one of them spoke.

"Hi there. Isn't this place just the business, eh?"

Clare looked up. "Sure." These were obviously the Canadians. If the accent hadn't given the speaker away, the plaid shirt she was wearing would have been a clue. *What was the term now, lumbersexual? Or did that only apply to men?*

"I'm Candice. This is Marguerite."

"Clare."

"Nice to meet you. Hey, don't I know you from somewhere?"

"I don't think so." Clare had been hoping to keep a low profile. But didn't it stand to reason that any lesbians who chose to come to Winterbourne House might be fans of the writer whose home it had once been?

"Nah. I know your face. It'll come to me. What do you think, Mags? She looks familiar, doesn't she?"

The other woman turned from the sideboard where she'd been pouring sherry into two glasses and gave Clare the once over. "Maybe." She handed a glass to her partner, then picked up a mince pie and shoved it into her mouth.

Clare studied the two women as they chose seats on the sofa facing the fire. The one who had introduced herself as Candice was average height, well proportioned—a polite way of saying fat but not obese—and her friendly face was framed with bushy sort-of-blonde hair. She did have a nice smile, and if Clare had to guess her profession she would choose nurse. Her monosyllabic partner was taller with sharper features, also a bit on the chunky side—either a teacher or a social worker. They both looked like outdoors types though. Probably used to wrestling grizzly bears when they took out the garbage.

"Have you been here before?" asked Candice. It was evidently up to her to keep the conversation going. The monosyllabic Mags had gone back to the sideboard to load more mince pies onto a plate.

"Once. A long time ago." Clare stared into the fire again. She didn't really want to dwell too much on that previous visit. It brought back bittersweet memories of the woman she had loved, the woman she had once thought would be her soul mate. No other lovers had quite lived up to the too brief time she spent with Kim Russell, her first real love affair.

"It's amazing. If we lived closer, we would come here every year. It's a bit of a pilgrimage for us, see. We're big fans of the Amy Ransom films. And to think most of the books they're based on were written here. Did you know there's a new TV series planned as well?"

"Mm." Clare nodded. Her cover was about to be blown. Short of wearing a wig and some prosthetic make-up, it wouldn't be long before these two recognised her. It was a relief when the door opened and two more guests came in, the two from the train station.

"Looks like this is the place to be," said the taller one. "Grab us a drink, Shel. I'm parched."

She plunked herself down on the only remaining chair. Shel was going to have to bunk up with the Canadians.

"Hi. You're Clare, aren't you? I'm JJ and this is Shelley. We're from Manchester. Where are you guys from?" She addressed this last question to the two women sitting on the sofa.

"Candice and Marguerite. We're from Vancouver. Well, I am. Mags is originally from Quebec, but I don't hold that against her." Her eyes twinkled when she said this.

Clare wondered how she'd hooked up with the morose looking Mags. The only other Canadian she had known well was Blake, and she had been an over-the-top extrovert, destroying any pre-conceived notions that

Canadians were polite and boring. Perfect for the part of Amy Ransom but annoying as hell to spend any length of time with. When people asked why it hadn't been an Australian actress playing the part, the answer always was that Blake could out-Aussie any Aussie.

"And where are you from, Clare? I'd guess from your accent that you're not from round here." Candice was clearly the spokesperson in that pairing.

"Sydney."

"Oh, wow! As in Australia? Awesome."

Clare had noticed during her meetings in London that the word "awesome" had migrated across the Atlantic, as with so many other Americanisms. She managed a brief smile. "Yeah, as in Australia."

"Hey! That's it. I know you now. You're that actress from AR4."

"And 7."

*Awesome*, thought Clare. *Two more words from Marguerite.* She just nodded. Most fans and critics just referred to the films by the eponymous character's initials and the number. No one could remember the titles. She recalled that Kim had always referred to the books that way as well. When Clare asked her why, she said it had started out as a joke between her and her editor with numbers one and two—toilet humour.

Before anyone else could pitch in, another arrival appeared in the doorway. An attractive blonde, on her own. Unless she had a reluctant lover in tow, Clare decided things were definitely looking up.

†

When Sally saw the group gathered around the fireplace, her first thought was to grab a glass and a couple of the freshly baked mince pies and retreat to her room. Sherry wasn't something she was prepared to drink, even to be sociable. Dipping into the bottle of Irish whiskey she'd brought for a medical emergency would be acceptable, though.

She recognised two of the women seated on the sofa. They had stopped their car on the way up the drive to ask if she wanted a lift to the house. She had declined, even though her rucksack was feeling heavier by the minute as the lane wound uphill. And the woman seated on the easy chair in the corner, well that was an unexpected bonus. This was going to make missing out on her usual round of Christmas parties in the city worthwhile. To top it all, she would be able to prove that cantankerous old woman wrong. On the long walk from the station, that had been foremost in her mind.

"This looks cosy. Mind if I join you?" She pulled up the upholstered stool next to the sideboard and placed it conveniently between the two from the car and the subject of her interest. "I'm Sally." She smiled brightly, letting her gaze travel around the room.

"Oh, yeah. We saw you walking up the lane. That's some trek from the main road."

"I walked from the station."

"What? Are you nuts? That's like five miles."

Sally figured the accent for American. "Well, it wasn't raining. That's always a bonus in this country. And living in London, a walk in the country is something to be treasured. I feel tons healthier already, just breathing in proper fresh air."

"I'm Candice and this is my partner Marguerite. That there's Shelley and," she pointed to the figure lounging in the other easy chair, "JJ from Manchester. And this, can you believe it, is Shay Finch from AR4 and 7. Sorry, hon, I don't remember your real name."

Sally thought she heard the woman in the chair next to her mutter, "They never do."

The door opened and the cute little red-haired butch who had greeted her at the front door came in carrying an armful of logs. She dumped them in the basket by the fireplace, sat herself down on the stone hearth and looked around at the group.

"Hi, I guess you've had time to introduce yourselves, so I won't ask you to do it again. This is the welcome speech but I'll keep it short, and if you have any questions, feel free to butt in. We like to keep things informal here. There is a Christmas programme that you will have seen, but please don't take it as written in stone. It's just a guide to activities which you can either take part in or not. The evening meals and buffet lunches will be supplied as advertised. Breakfast, however, is up to you. The cupboards in the kitchen are labelled so you can find what you need. One of us will be up early enough to get the coffee pot going. There's also a selection of teas. Fresh eggs and bacon are available if you want to cook your own. We just ask that you clean up after yourselves and leave the place tidy. My partner, Gaby, is nine months pregnant but still insists on taking care of the catering. She won't let me anywhere near the kitchen when she's cooking, but she might be amenable to letting you help out if you feel so inclined.

"And if you want a change of scene, we can recommend the pub in the village. It's run by two good friends of ours, Toby and Mark. They'll be joining us for the festivities on Christmas day, as will Felicity and Rose who run the stables, and our two friends and business partners from London, Ade and Rita. You'll also come across Gaby's parents at some point, Teresa and Guido. They've been here a number of times so they're also a good source of information. Any questions?"

Sally glanced around at her fellow guests and wondered who would be the first to ask a question. The instructions they had received after making reservations had been very detailed but no one ever took time to read such things properly.

The one called JJ spoke up. "When can we use the pool?"

A mental tick. *Yes, that was on the sheet.*

Wil Tyler didn't blink. She just said calmly, "There's a key on a hook inside the back door. You can use it anytime. We ask that you lock up the chalet and return the key. It's kept locked, not because we usually have any trouble with local kids wanting to get in, but if anyone did we would be considered negligent if we left it open. There are towels in the cupboard down there. Just leave them in the laundry basket when you're finished."

"We booked a riding session online." Candice ventured.

"Yes, that's right. I'll be going out with you. Just turn up at the stables about ten minutes before and we'll sort you out with riding hats. Oh, and dress warmly. Also, for anyone else visiting the stables, there are two dogs in residence, Daisy and Raffi. You might also see them roaming the grounds. They're Labradors and very friendly but please don't feed them. Even with all the exercise they get around here, it's an effort to keep their weight down." She stood and gave the group another once over. "Well, if you're all okay for now, I'll leave you to it. Don't eat too many mince pies. It's champagne and canapés in half an hour."

When she closed the door behind her, Candice sighed and said, "Well, isn't she just the cutest thing. I could listen to her talk all day."

*And which part of small town America are you from?* Sally wondered. She glanced at the woman slouched in the chair next to her who was looking like she wanted to blend into the background. Getting her out of Candice's clutches would be Sally's first task. It made her job easier. She would be able to gain her trust. Yes, she thought, the old woman was going to be made to eat her words.

†

After doing her "welcome the guests" speech in the lounge, Wil walked back down to the stables to give Felicity and Rose a hand with getting the horses settled for the night. Sandy, their hired help, had done the sensible thing and taken two weeks off to holiday in the sun. Madeira, of all places. They must be paying her too much.

With the chores done, Wil sat down on the hay bale at the end of the block and listened to the horses shuffling around in their stalls. Paddy's head was hanging out over her half door. "You've had your treats for today, greedy guts. No more until tomorrow."

Paddy snickered and shook her head, as if she understood, and turned back into her stall to munch on her mundane dinner of hay.

The mare was the first horse Wil had really considered her own since taking ownership of the estate. Kim's horse, Glenmorangie, had accepted her as a substitute eventually. His career as a stud had been cut short when he died of a fever, and Paddy was his only offspring. Wil always thought he died because he missed Kim.

She missed Kim, too. The writer had been there for her during the worst periods in Wil's life. She just wished Kim had been there to share in the best ones, too. Although she wasn't sure that Kim would have put being a grandmother at the top of that list.

Not for the first time that month, Wil was wondering why they hadn't just closed for the holiday period. But Gaby had convinced her that she wanted to carry on working until the child was born. She would take a break then. But Gaby's idea of a break was likely to be only half a day before she would want to be doing something again. The whirlwind named Gabriella and the love of Wil's life.

Meeting Gaby had been a revelation. Whether she'd wanted to admit it to herself or not, the enduring images from her impressionable teenage years were of her mother's intense relationship with Kim and their fall out. Wil had witnessed many emotionally charged scenes between the two of them. She idolised Kim and had been devastated by the change in the writer after her mother's death. And then there was the less-than-tranquil nature of Kim's relationship with Grace, the woman Wil felt was responsible for destroying the writer's life completely. Her own love life had suffered as a consequence. She would never let anyone affect her like that; or so she'd thought until she met this gorgeous creature, Gaby, unexpectedly.

...It had been a hot day in Rome and Wil had spent most of it in the university's library looking up references for the paper she was writing about the Etruscan people. Someone she'd met at a cafe had invited her to a party that evening and she almost didn't go. As it was, she spent most of the evening leaning against a wall, watching people she didn't know smoke and drink their way into oblivion. She sipped at a glass of red wine and refused two offers of badly wrapped spliffs. It really wasn't her scene. Gabriella arrived with a group and at first Wil thought she was partnered up with one of them, but after a while they started to mingle separately. Wil finished her wine and decided to make a discreet exit. As she'd spoken to no one, she wasn't likely to be missed. Standing outside the apartment building, she had just inhaled a welcome breath of fresh air when a voice behind her asked, in Italian, if she was leaving already. She turned around to find the dark-haired beauty she'd noticed earlier watching her from the doorway. Not trusting herself to speak, she simply nodded. Gabriella came up to her, took her hand, and asked her to please stay.

That evening they just talked. They met again in the following days, going for walks, sitting in cafés. Wil didn't think it would go any further than that although she really fancied the woman. But she knew she would be heading back to England soon and didn't want to start something that would end with a tearful separation and empty promises to keep in touch. Then Gaby asked Wil to go with her to see her parents. It was a family gathering for her younger brother's birthday and she said she didn't want to go on her own.

Several surprising things happened that weekend. First of all, Gaby's family welcomed her wholeheartedly. Secondly, they obviously expected she and Gaby would sleep together and put them in the same bedroom. Wil hadn't known what to do that first night. She waited until Gaby went to the bathroom, undressed hastily and crept under the covers. Gaby had laughed when she came back and saw her there. She had performed an extremely seductive striptease and jumped into bed. By the time they were on the motorbike, travelling back to Rome at the end of two days of family celebrations, Wil was in love.

She suffered through sleepless nights worrying about the problems of continuing a long-distance relationship, but she knew the holiday was coming to an end. Although Kim had encouraged her to make the trip, she was also concerned about Kim's state of mind. The writer hadn't responded to Wil's last email and, failing to reach Kim at Winterbourne by phone, she decided to tell Gaby she had to go. She promised to be back as soon as possible. Gaby surprised her again by saying she would come with her; she had always wanted to see London. They stopped in Turin, initially planning to stay the night, and Wil tried again to reach Kim with no success. Then she rang Ade.

The drive through France had broken all records. Wil didn't remember much about riding almost non-stop until they reached the Channel tunnel. Gaby had been brilliant, not complaining once about lack of sleep or being saddle-sore from the long ride. She even made sure that when they did stop they had something to eat and drink. Dozing briefly during the quick trip on the train through the tunnel, Wil woke up at Waterloo Station hoping that it had all been a bad dream…

Shaking herself mentally, Wil stood up and brushed herself down. She had a few sugar lumps left in her pocket and stopped by Paddy's stall to give her a final treat for the night.

"Rest well, my friend," she said, stroking the long silky nose. "We're going out for a long ride tomorrow with the visitors. Your favourite trail." With a final caress of the mare's silky nose, she left the stables and headed back up to the house. Time to get washed and changed again and start pouring out the champagne.

†

"We don't have to dress for dinner, do we?" Mags asked from her prone position on the bed, arm draped over her eyes.

"It's not that kind of place." Candice finished applying the eyeliner and checked her hair again before turning back to face her partner. "What's wrong, sweetheart? Are you not feeling well?"

"No. Just a bit tired, I guess." Mags sat up and swung her feet off the bed. She wandered into the bathroom and closed the door firmly.

Candice stared at the door. It was best to leave her for now. Apart from her other problem, she was probably feeling a bit homesick. They had been away for three weeks and it was the first Christmas they had spent away from their families. Usually they alternated each year, one Christmas with her folks on Vancouver Island, and one with Marguerite's in their chalet north of Montreal. This year would have been the chalet, which usually involved hours of cross-country skiing after a fresh, crisp snowfall.

She hoped the surroundings of Winterbourne would help bring Mags out of herself. The horse riding would be fun and they should take a look at the swimming pool. Experience over the last two years had shown that exercise was often the best form of therapy.

†

The dining room was all set. Wil checked the table again. They were just using one large round table tonight for the six guests. She would serve the meal, and once the guests were settled with their main course, she would join Gaby in the kitchen. Felicity and Rose had invited Teresa and Guido to eat with them at the Lodge. Wil suspected they were planning a bridge session. It had become a fixture whenever Gaby's parents visited. Serious business, they played for money. The first time the Italians visited and Felicity discovered they played the card game, Wil had warned her about fleecing her in-laws. After that initial round, Felicity told her that she and Rose were more in danger of losing their home. They were going to have to up their game.

Wil placed the jug of ice water in the centre of the table. The red wine had been breathing for a while and it was time to open the white. Lighting the candles was the last job before she was ready to let the guests know they could come in and seat themselves.

†

Clare looked around at the table in dismay. She had hoped their hosts would be joining them for dinner. Excusing herself from the lounge after Wil gave her welcoming speech, she had wandered out to look at the swimming pool and considered the possibility of enticing Sally into a midnight swim. She thought she could avoid the Canadian woman's attention, but during the before-dinner drinks, Candice cornered her again to ask what it was like working with Gemma Blake. Curious Candice was leading up to asking about Blake's accident when Morbid Mags came to the rescue, unexpectedly, by dragging her partner away to look at a picture in the hall.

Now she had a choice of sitting between Surly Shelley and Jaunty Jill, the couple having separated themselves for some reason, or next to Curious Candice. Having given nicknames to the other guests, she wondered what she should call herself. Cautious Clare, maybe.

First impressions shouldn't be trusted. She knew that, in theory, from her work. The film industry was awash with people of all types. Maybe, by Christmas day, this disparate group would all have bonded. Maybe Wil had some party games lined up. Ice breakers. Maybe she should cut her losses and head back up to London, check in at the Ritz or the Dorchester, and spoil herself.

She smiled at Shelley and sat down next to her, deciding the surly one was less likely to ask questions. Sally hadn't arrived yet, and for some reason Clare suspected the Londoner was gearing up to give her a grilling. A midnight swim on her own was looking like a more attractive prospect.

At least she could look forward to the nightcap in the study. Ade and Rita were arriving later and Wil had invited her to come and join them.

Clare recalled her previous visit, when she had arrived too late to attend Kim's funeral. But she had wanted to see the place she had heard so much about, the place that held Kim's heart. She hadn't known there were so many places called Winterbourne in England, and after fruitless journeys to first somewhere near Bristol and then Birmingham, she had called Ade McPherson, Kim's best friend.

...Following the hair-raising drive from London with two women she didn't know, she had walked in on Wil and Gaby who had obviously been making love in front of the fire in the study. She hadn't met Wil before but she was exactly as Kim had described her.

It had taken her most of the next day to get Wil on her own; the girl seemed to be avoiding her. However, she eventually agreed to show her Kim's favourite walk through the woods. They took the path by the stream through lush foliage and came to a small clearing with a stone-built fire pit in the middle. Strategically placed logs formed a circle around it.

Wil sat down and motioned Clare to do the same. She had been silent throughout the walk. Now she asked, "Clare, why are you here? Really?"

Clare looked at her, moved by the pain she saw in those bewitching green eyes. There were so many questions she wanted answers for, but she wasn't sure how far she could push without hurting Wil further. Mostly she was curious about the other two women who had featured so prominently in Kim's life—Wil's mother, Ginny, and the lover Kim had come back to, Grace Green. It seemed best to start with talking about Kim.

"Wil, I understand that this may seem strange to you, me turning up like this. But, Kim was special. No one's ever made love to me the way she did. I wanted her to stay with me, but she said her heart was here. She talked about this place a lot, and about you. She wanted to give you a proper home."

"So why did she push me away? At the time when she most needed someone, she told me to go away for six months."

"She wrote to me about that. Not that she was ill. But that she wanted you to experience life. You're young, you have a lot of time ahead of you."

"I wanted to have more time…with Kim."

"She wouldn't want a nursemaid and she wouldn't have wanted you to see her deteriorating. I would guess she wanted you to remember her as she was before the illness took hold."

Wil sat still for so long that Clare thought she would have to prise her off the log. But finally, she stood, brushed herself off and suggested they walk on.

"I've always wondered," Wil said eventually, "why Amy Ransom was so popular in Australia. Kim had never set foot in the country before that trip. She knew sod all about the place."

"Well, she could tell a good story. So we sort of forgave her any discrepancies in terminology. Anyway, she said she'd got enough background to get by from *The Thorn Birds* and *The Flying Doctors* series."

"*The Thorn Birds*…I can't believe Kim would have sat still through that crap."

"Yeah, well, must have been the eye candy…she said your mother reminded her of Meggie."

"She talked to you about my mother?"

"Yeah, she talked so much about her it was like having three in the bed at times."

"And why the fuck would you put up with that?"

Clare stopped on the path, and made Wil face her. "Because I loved her."

"So, why didn't you stay together?"

"She felt guilty about Grace, and she wanted to be here for you. I have family in Melbourne. It just wasn't the right time, for either of us. We kept in touch and I suppose, like you, I thought we had time on our side to get together again. But we didn't, did we?" Clare was close to tears again.

"She might as well have stayed. You know, when she got back from the film premiere in San Francisco, Grace had changed the locks on the London house and sent all her belongings to Winterbourne?"

"I didn't know that!"

"Grace had somehow found out about your relationship. I suspect someone on the film crew told her. She was pretty high profile by then. It may even have been that bitch, Hannah, she took up with. Hannah Styles. Kim commented that it sounded like a good name for a hairdresser. That was the worst insult she could come up with," Wil said, with a hint of bitterness in her voice. "Anyway that relationship didn't last long. Grace kept coming back."

"Kim was pretty hard to resist."

"Sure. She still loved Grace, though. They would argue, spend weeks not seeing each other, then fuck like rabbits when they did meet up. Grace would go back to work, and when she wasn't around, Kim would hit the bottle. Didn't her drinking bother you?"

Clare realised she didn't have an answer to that. Looking back at the times she spent with Kim, she only remembered the laughter and the loving. No relationships since had ever measured up…

Opening her eyes, the scene with Wil in the woods vanished. So much time had passed. Clare needed to let go of those memories if she wanted to find someone to share her life with. At forty-five, her single status was feeling less desirable by the year.

†

Finding herself sitting opposite her target at dinner wasn't working out as Sally had planned. She had thought the couples were likely to sit together. It was her own fault she hadn't been there to grab the seat next to Clare. She was last to arrive in the dining room because after the champagne and nibbles, she had helped Wil clear away—curious to meet the mysterious Gabriella whom she knew was a partner in the business.

The sight of the dark-haired beauty hovering by the stove had been breathtaking. Well, she didn't blame Wil Tyler for keeping her out of view. The fact that she was heavily pregnant only enhanced her natural good looks.

"Thanks, Sally. You can put the trays down there," Wil said, pointing to a space on the counter.

"This is a wonderful kitchen," Sally offered, wanting to prolong the visit. It was very well equipped with lots of space to accommodate the large wooden table with six chunky chairs around it.

"Yeah, well, it suits its purpose. Anyway, you'll have time to explore when you come down for breakfast."

Taking that as a discreet dismissal, Sally left and found her way back to the dining room.

She had just sat down and unfolded her napkin when Candice jumped in with her first question. "Do you like horse riding?"

"No."

"Oh, I thought it was the main attraction for coming here. JJ and Shelley don't ride either."

"No, the main attraction is that it's for lesbians," JJ countered quickly.

"So, if you don't want to ride, what are you going to do here?" Candice wasn't to be put off easily.

"Well, I like walking and the pool sounds inviting. Has anyone been over to have a look at it, yet?" Sally helped herself to water from the jug on the table.

"No. We haven't had time. But I'm planning on an early morning swim."

"Good for you. I'm planning on a lie in."

Wil, arriving with their starters, interrupted them. Everyone made polite murmurs about how wonderful it looked, and started eating. Everyone except Clare.

When Sally looked up from tasting the creamy mushrooms, she noticed that the actress seemed to have zoned out. She was staring at the chandelier with the strangest look on her face.

"Hey, Earth to Shay," Candice called out.

"It's Clare," she said. "My name's Clare."

"Oh, right, of course. Sorry."

Sally gave her what she hoped was a sympathetic look. "Are you going to eat any of that?"

Clare looked down at the untouched food in front of her. "No, I guess I had too many canapés. I'm saving myself for the main course." She took a sip of her red wine. "Would anyone like to finish this off?"

For the first time since she'd sat down, Sally heard Marguerite speak.

"Sure, I'll take it if you don't want it."

They exchanged plates across the table.

Wil came back in just as Marguerite finished the last of the mushrooms. She cleared the plates efficiently, checked if they needed more wine and said she'd be back shortly with their main courses.

Sally leant back, sipping at her white wine, which was surprisingly good. She hadn't expected much from either the wine selection or the cuisine at this venue. In a place full of lesbians, she had been prepared for a diet of real ale and lentils. So far it compared favourably with some of her favourite city restaurants.

"We've got a great view from our room," Candice enthused. "The woods do look inviting for walks, if that's what you like, Sally."

"I expect it will be nice. One of my windows faces the drive, but I've already done that walk. It was very pleasant though." Sally realised she was babbling. Really, she needed to get a grip. It was like an episode of *Time Team*. She had three days to excavate the hidden secrets of this household. This first evening didn't really count, she was just getting the lay of the land, and the real chances to start digging would come the next day. Getting Clare on her own was her mission for the morning. With Candice and Mags out riding, JJ and Shelley off somewhere on their own, she could surely manage to corner the enigmatic actress. Sally had caught a glimmer of interest in her eyes when she'd first arrived in the lounge.

†

"I would like to get there in one piece, Adriana."

"I thought you were asleep." Ade glanced over at Rita who was gripping the sides of her seat, feet braced against the floor. The clipped tone of voice and use of her full name meant her wife was well and truly stressed.

"Keep your eyes on the road, for God's sake."

"Keep your hair on, love. I've driven this route a million times. It's dark. If anyone's coming the other way I'll see their headlights in good time."

Rita didn't relax her grip on the seat until they turned into the drive.

"So, what's going on with the kids?" Ade asked as she parked the car in front of the house next to a rental vehicle.

"I don't know," Rita sighed. "I've had Gabs on the phone every day, in tears."

"I've tried to talk to Wil but I think she's deliberately ignoring my calls." Ade popped open the boot and unfurled herself from the front seat. She loved driving the Jag but it was a bugger to get in and out of. Even with the seat as far back as she could get it, and still reach the steering wheel, her six-foot frame felt squashed.

Rita stretched as she emerged more gracefully from the other side of the car. She was almost as tall as Ade and also felt the need to move her lower limbs to get the feeling back. Ade passed her the bag full of presents and took out their suitcase. When they had discussed coming down for Christmas, it was initially only going to be for a few nights. But a sense of something troubling the relationship of their two young friends had grown over the past week, so they had packed for the contingency of staying longer if it proved necessary.

"Well, I don't know about you, but I'm ready for that drink Wil owes me for not answering my calls."

"I'll settle for a nice cup of herbal tea."

Rita opened the door into the hallway and was immediately entranced by the large tree that filled most of the space. "Oh, that's wonderful! I told Gaby the red and silver would work."

Ade glanced at the decorated tree. "Yeah. Nice. Look, I'm going to get changed. Will you be joining us for a drink?" She started up the stairs.

Rita followed slowly. "Maybe. I'll check on Gaby first."

Setting the suitcase on the bench under the window in their room, Ade located the sweatpants left in a drawer from their last visit. She changed out of the jeans she'd been wearing and discarded her leather jacket. Rita had already disappeared to put the kettle on. She found her in the kitchenette looking through a selection of herb teas.

"I think the rosehip will be good for both of us."

"I'm not drinking it."

"It's for me and Gaby. You go and find out what's up with Wil."

Ade wrapped her arms around her and nuzzled the sensitive area behind her ear. "Love you," she murmured.

"Yeah, I know." Rita wiggled her backside into Ade's groin. "But save it for later, stud. Gabs and I have some serious girl talk to catch up on." She moved out of Ade's grasp and retrieved two mugs from the cupboard by the sink.

The kettle boiled and Rita waited a few moments for the bubbling to settle before pouring the hot water onto the bags in the two mugs on the counter.

"Smells disgusting. Are you sure that's good for a pregnant woman?"

"It most certainly is. Now go. And don't drink too much. We have some catching up to do as well."

Ade was still smiling with that lingering thought as she walked back down the stairs to the ground floor.

When she opened the door to the study, she was surprised to hear voices. She'd thought Wil would be alone. And the identity of her companion was another surprise. They had only met that one time fifteen years earlier, but she would have recognised the actress anywhere. Apart from her role in two of the Amy Ransom films, Ade was a fan of the martial arts movies Clare had also starred in.

"Clare! Oh my God! Where have you sprung from?"

The tall Australian with her Wonder Woman style body didn't seem to have aged at all. Her wavy blonde hair was cut shorter, but apart from that, the normal ravages of time seemed to have passed her by. She jumped up from the couch and met Ade in the middle of the room for a hug.

"Good to see you, too."

"Well, I do think one of you could have let me know the evil one was here?" Ade looked at Wil who was standing behind Clare, waiting her turn for a hug. When she'd released Clare, she pulled Wil close and was alarmed to feel her body trembling. "We'll catch up later," Ade whispered in her ear.

Clare had seated herself again on the end of the couch closest to the fire. "I resemble that remark," she said with a smile.

"Sorry, I should have given you your full title—That Evil Bitch."

"That's better. I've had to put up with being called Shay for most of the evening by Creeping Candy."

Wil laughed and Ade looked bemused. "Who?"

"One of the guests," Wil said. She looked over at Clare. "Do you have nicknames for all of them, or is it just Candice who's pissing you off?"

Ade poured herself a drink. At least Wil had remembered to put out a glass for her next to the bottle of Jameson's on the table.

"Well, let's see. There's Candice's partner, Morose Mags and the other couple, Sulky Shelley and Jumping Jane. When I saw them get off the train, I thought they would be coming here." Clare paused to take a sip of her drink before continuing. "I think Simpering Sally fancies me, so I'll go easy on her for now."

They all laughed. Ade sipped at her drink and enjoyed the warmth of the liquid as it spread through her mouth and down her throat.

"Sounds like you've got your hands full, Wil. I thought Gaby's parents were here, too."

"Yeah, they arrived a few days ago. They're at the Lodge tonight, taking money off Felicity and Rose. I think Guido prefers it down there as this house is a smoke-free zone."

"So, what are you doing here, Clare?"

"Talking to some people about a TV series."

Ade didn't miss the look that passed between Wil and Clare.

"You can't be serious. I mean, with what happened to Blake…"

"They're deadly serious, but they want to change the focus. They have the idea that Kim left some unfinished drafts with Shay as the main character."

Wil put her head in her hands. "Bloody Thelma. I should never have trusted her."

"What's Thelma got to do with it? She's retired, isn't she?"

"Sort of."

"What do you mean, sort of?" Ade finished her drink in one gulp and reached out to pour herself another shot. Wil and Clare were drinking red wine and still had half a bottle to go.

"Well, when they closed down their publishing business, Richard headed off to the apartment in Paris that he and Eddy had bought some years before as their retirement home. Thelma went on a round-the-world cruise, and when she came back she set herself up as a literary agent." Wil poured out more wine for herself and Clare.

"And what's that got to do with anything?" Ade asked.

"I know she looks like Robin Williams in drag, but she's a smooth operator. She turned up here not long after we started the renovations, and after some initial flannel, asked me if Kim had left any unfinished works. They thought Kim had been working on number ten. I just told her I would think about it. Anyway, as you know, when I finally got around to looking at Kim's computer files, I did find Amy number ten. And it was complete." Wil leant back on the couch with her eyes closed.

Ade looked at her young friend in sympathy. Even after all this time, Wil still found it hard to talk about Kim.

Taking a few deep breaths, Wil continued. "I gave Thelma two disks. As well as the novel, there were some files which I thought were just background notes relating to the story, character sketches, that kind of thing. Turns out they were a bit more than that. She had drafted outlines for several more novels, with Shay Finch as the main character. Thelma did tell me she had found these on the disk but at the time said they weren't much use, just bits and pieces of ideas. Maybe she hasn't found her fifty shades of anything yet, so she's now decided to enhance her retirement fund by selling these to the highest bidder."

"Wow! Wil, you should have told me."

"I didn't think it would amount to anything. I'd put it out of my mind, until Clare showed up today and told me they want her to star in the production."

They all sat, quietly sipping their drinks and gazing into the fireplace. Ade was wondering how she could politely ask Clare to leave so she and Wil could have the heart-to-heart that was evidently needed. The actress topped up her glass of wine, and Ade thought she was settling in, but was pleased when Clare stood.

"I'll take this to my room. Great to see you both. I guess we can catch up more over the next few days, but right now I'm bushed."

As soon as she'd closed the door, Ade moved over to sit next to Wil. "So, what's up, kiddo?"

"I don't know. She won't talk to me."

"It's probably just hormones. I've heard pregnancy does weird things to you."

"Yeah. But she doesn't have to cut me out. I want to be supportive. I might as well send Mark up here to be with her."

Mark was the sperm donor and therefore the biological father. Ade didn't know him very well, but she knew that Gaby and Wil had become close friends with the pub landlords when they had taken over the Good Shepherd in the village ten years before. Winterbourne Village had become something of a gay magnet.

"Look, you're probably both worn out. You've had a busy year and now this."

"I tried to tell her we should close for Christmas but you know how stubborn she can be."

Ade squeezed her knee. "You're as stubborn as each other. Rita's having a chat with her. She'll find out what's going on."

"So, why can she talk to Rita and not me?" Wil looked close to tears.

"Because…well, just because." Ade pulled the smaller woman into a one armed embrace and held onto her while she cried.

After a few minutes, Wil pulled herself away and swiped at her wet face with her sleeve. She went over to the fire and moved the charred remains of the logs about with the poker. "This is supposed to be our child. And right now I don't feel like I'm part of it."

"I don't think that's unusual. Gaby's body has been changing over the last eight months. Birth mothers have all that time to adapt to it."

"I've seen her body changing. Don't you think I've had to adapt as well?"

"Are you sure you're not just feeling jealous because you're not the focus of her attention anymore? Because if that's the case you better get used to it. A baby is for life…"

"Not just for Christmas. I know." Wil sighed. She looked at Ade from her position crouched by the hearth. "I better go up. Got another long day tomorrow. And first on the agenda is a ride with Candice and Marguerite. I'm not sure either one of them has ridden before." She stood up and set the fireguard in place.

Ade gave her another brief hug. "It'll be okay."

Wil just nodded and went out to do her final check of the other fires and unplug the lights on the tree. Ade sipped her drink slowly, watching the dying embers in the fireplace.

## Chapter Two

### Christmas Eve

The blank page stared up at her from her laptop screen. Sally gathered her thoughts slowly. She had been down to the kitchen and, pleased to have it to herself, made a mug of tea and two slices of toast and marmalade. Back in her room, she sipped at the tea and considered what she knew and what steps she needed to take to learn more.

There was no shortage of sources. First there was Wil Tyler, Kim's adopted daughter. Tapping into her memories of life with the writer during her formative years would be fascinating. She would have been witness not only to her own mother's affair with Kim, but also the tempestuous but long-term relationship with the now famous television presenter, Grace Green. That was something that needed exploring. She hadn't been able to get close to Ms Green. The woman was surrounded by too many minders.

Then there was Felicity Evans. Not just a stable hand. When Kim first took over the estate, the horsewoman had been like a housekeeper, a protective Mrs Danvers. And a few years before her death, Kim had given her the Lodge and the land around the riding stables, as well as most of the stock. So they had obviously been close.

And as an extra bonus, there were two more sources she hadn't bargained for. She could have found Ade McPherson, Kim's closest friend, in London. But now Ade was going to be here, the person who had known Kim well before she became a household name.

First on the list to tackle though would be Clare Finlayson. What had brought Clare back here after so many years? The presence of the Australian actress was more than a lucky coincidence. Sally's limited funds wouldn't have stretched to a trip to the other side of the world. The newspaper reports she'd dug out from the archives gave sketchy hints of a love affair, plus rumours that this liaison was what had caused the final rift between the writer and Grace Green. And yet it seemed she was a favoured guest. Sally had spotted her going into the room marked "Private" when she'd returned from the toilet after dinner. She mentioned this to the others in the lounge as she rejoined them for coffee, and JJ said that Clare had greeted Wil as a long lost friend at the train station.

She recalled the glint in the old woman's eyes when Sally told her she was coming down here. Another source, if Sally could get her to talk. After all, the old woman had been Kim's editor.

She typed up her notes between bites of toast. This was rich. If she played it right she could get more than enough information in the next three days.

†

The cupboard held a variety of cereals.

"Wow, Mags. Weetabix. I haven't had one of these since I was a kid." Candice pulled the box out. Neither had anyone else, it seemed. The box was pristine, unopened. "Do you want one?"

Marguerite looked up from examining the contents of the bread bin. "No. I'll stick to toast."

"There's eggs and bacon in the fridge. I'll cook some up if you want."

"*Non, merci.*"

Candice knew the signs weren't good when her partner slipped into her native tongue. She hadn't emerged from the dark mood she'd been in since they arrived. It was like a large black cloud hanging over her head. Candice didn't think Mags would appreciate it if she asked how long the chicken of depression was staying. It didn't look like a return for the bluebird of happiness any time soon. Sometimes making a joke of it could relieve her own feelings of despair when Mags sank into a depressive phase.

The fruit bowl on the table held several ripened bananas. Candice took one and sliced half onto her Weetabix. It took her a minute to find the milk. Small glass bottles with round foil tops. She didn't know they existed outside of old British films. Milk at home came out of a carton or a plastic bag.

After the first mouthful she remembered why she hadn't eaten the cereal in so many years. It had the taste and texture of wet cardboard. A sprinkling of sugar helped the taste and the banana was nice. She decided that tomorrow she would cook eggs and bacon, even if they were having the large Christmas lunch a few hours later.

Candice and Mags were just finishing their respective breakfasts when a dark-haired, heavily pregnant woman came into the kitchen. It didn't take much deduction to know who she was.

"Hi. I'm Candice," she said brightly. "And this is Marguerite."

The woman smiled at them, a beautiful smile that would light up any room. "Gabriella," she said. Turning the full force of her radiant smile on Mags, she said, "*Êtes-vous Française?*"

Mags still had her mouth open and recovered with a visible effort at being addressed by this vision. "*Oui. Je suis Française. Êtes-vous, Italien?*"

"*Si. Da Roma.*"

"*Bellissima!*" Mags waved her arms around expansively. Candice wasn't sure if she meant the house, Rome or Gabriella. Maybe all three. She'd certainly come out of her shell.

"Um. Nice to meet you Gabriella. We're going for a ride this morning. Hope we'll see you later." Candice got up and took her bowl to the sink. She started to run the water into the washing bowl.

"Leave those. I'll take care of them."

"Oh, but we should clean up after ourselves. I'm sure you've got a lot to do today."

"It's no problem. *Prego.*"

Candice recognised the command underlying the polite tone. "Sure thing. We'll get out of your hair. Come on, Mags." She watched as her partner gave Gabriella a brilliant smile, one that she hadn't seen for three days.

"*Avere una buona giornata*, Marguerite."

"*Grazie.*"

*What was that all about?* Candice wondered as they returned to their room to get dressed for riding.

†

Wil woke to unfamiliar sounds outside the bedroom door—a crash, followed by loud swearing and muffled laughter. Then she remembered. Ade and Rita, trying to be quiet. She reached over and found only an empty space in the bed. It wasn't even warm. Gaby had managed to avoid any early morning intimacies, yet again.

The room was freezing cold. Gaby liked it that way these days as her body seemed overheated all the time. Wil braced herself before throwing back the duvet and planting her feet on the rug next to the bed. She shrugged into the sweatshirt she'd left on the floor and found her jeans in a similar heap not far away. Time for a shower later. She needed to make it to the bathroom first for a pee, and then see if the two urbanites had managed to make coffee.

When she emerged into the kitchenette, they were sitting at opposite ends of the small table but she could see their feet touching.

"Hey, sleepyhead. We didn't wake you, did we?" Ade grinned up at her, hands wrapped around her mug.

"You'd wake the dead trying to be quiet."

"Coffee's on."

"That's the only reason we're speaking right now."

Rita grabbed her as she passed the table and pulled her close. "Come here, sweetness. You haven't even said hello to me yet."

"Hello."

"Who got up on the wrong side of the bed this morning?"

"She who got up from an empty bed this morning, as usual." Wil stated flatly. She gave Rita's arm a squeeze and wriggled out of her grasp.

Pouring herself a mug of coffee, she didn't need to turn around to know there were looks passing between the other two.

"Wil, come and sit down." Rita was using her schools inspector voice, and Wil knew better than to ignore her instruction. "Ade, make some toast."

Wil smiled to herself as Ade jumped up quickly to do as she was told. Sitting down in the chair that placed her between her two friends, she sipped coffee and waited for Rita's pronouncement.

"I talked to Gaby last night. She thinks you're having an affair."

"What!" Coffee flew out of Wil's mouth. She swallowed the remaining liquid and looked into Rita's concerned brown eyes.

"She thinks you're turned off by her looking the size of a house."

"That's just...just crazy. I mean, who am I supposed to be having an affair with? And when would I have time?"

"I know. It's just the way her mind's working at the moment. I tried to reassure her last night but she was too emotionally wound up. You need to talk to her."

"I've tried, believe me. She just shuts me out."

"Well, I've told her to talk to you. And she listens to me."

"Yeah. Still, we've got a busy few days. There's never going to be a good time."

"Good thing I have a cunning plan, then."

Ade slid a plate of toast in front of her, buttered and covered in raspberry jam. She took Wil's coffee cup and refilled it before sitting down again. "So, listen up, bud. This is your mission…"

"Shut up, Ade." Rita gave her the stare that put the frighteners on head teachers in schools up and down the country. She turned back to Wil. "You're only going to have to be patient for a wee bit longer. I've convinced her to take the evening off."

"She'll never do that. This evening's meal, it's a big production. And there's all the prep for tomorrow as well."

"I've gone over the menu with her. It's nothing that Rose and I can't handle. We'll draft in Felicity and Toby as well. And Teresa's just dying to help out. Guido can pour wine."

"So, what's Gaby going to be doing?"

"She's going to be having dinner here, with you."

"With me?"

"Yes, honey. You're going to have a date."

"Yeah, so don't blow it, kid." Ade grinned at her.

Wil looked from one to the other. "A date?"

"Yes. When was the last time the two of you had any quality time to yourselves?"

Wil gulped down some coffee. "A date." She managed a weak grin. "I guess it's worth a try."

"Of course it is. Now eat your breakfast. You've got a busy day ahead of you." Rita got up from the table and carried her mug and plate over to the sink. "You can do the washing up, Ade. I've got work to do downstairs."

As soon as Rita had disappeared, Ade said, "Don't you just love her when she's in bossy bitch mode?"

Wil grunted as she chewed on her toast.

Ade continued, "I know you're going to be busy today. And no doubt it will take you most of the afternoon to decide what to wear for your *date*. But I would like a few minutes of your time to have a look at next year's schedule. We also need to update the Facebook page and the website."

"Okay. But while I'm out riding this morning, could you do me a favour?"

"What's that?"

"Well, I need to do this date thing properly, don't I? Could you find somewhere that sells flowers and buy a bouquet, no expense spared? And make sure Gaby doesn't see them."

"Of course. I'm on shopping duty anyway. Reet's given me a list of supplies to get today."

"Rather you than me. It'll be hell out there. Last twelve hours before Christmas."

"Don't think I'll have any problem." Ade stood up and stretched. Her hands could touch the ceiling. She grinned at Wil as she left. "Catch you later, kid."

Wil finished her toast. Checking the wall clock, she had time for a shower before going down to the stables to meet the guests. She would need another one when she got back, but she liked to start the day feeling clean.

Letting the hot water cascade over her head and shoulders, Wil found her thoughts drifting back to the times she'd spent with Ade and Rita. They would always regard her as a child. Or maybe a stray animal that needed looking after. During her university years, she'd crashed at their place on weekends. It was safer than going home to listen to the fights between Kim and Grace. Rita would try to feed her, and Ade would take her out to pubs. Wil wasn't much of a drinker, not after witnessing the effects, first on her mother and then Kim. But she and Ade would talk, set the world to rights, and she knew that those weekends had been her lifeline to sanity.

Wil made it down to the stables with ten minutes to spare. Time enough to check in with Felicity. If Ade and Rita were doing parent impersonations, Felicity and Rose could be considered grandmothers. Although Felicity would have placed her headfirst and none too gently into a pile of manure if she ever ventured that observation out loud.

"So, hot date tonight?" were Felicity's first words to her, approaching as Wil saddled up Paddy.

"Are there no secrets around here?"

"Not where your love life is concerned."

"Oh, great." Wil picked an apple out of the barrel by the tack room door. She gave it to Paddy to munch before putting the bridle on her head. "So, did you win any money last night?"

"Not a chance with those two sharks." Felicity shook her head. "If we'd been playing strip poker, we'd have been down to our knickers in no time."

Wil laughed. "Now that I would like to see."

"No you wouldn't."

The sound of a car approaching made them both look across the yard.

"Looks like your punters have arrived."

"Couldn't they have walked from the house?"

"Of course not. They're Americans. They don't walk."

"Actually, they're from Canada."

"Same diff."

"Better not say that in their hearing." Wil waved as the two women got out of the car. It seemed they had taken her advice to dress warmly a little too literally. Candice was wrapped up as if heading out for a skiing expedition.

†

Gaby was in the kitchen when Clare arrived. She had decided to hunt down a cup of coffee before heading out for a walk, and she was pleased to have avoided encountering any of the other guests. Wil's partner, busying herself with checking a list of groceries, didn't seem inclined to conversation. Clare helped herself to coffee from the pot and made a quick exit. She stood out on the terrace and breathed in the fresh, crisp country air. Clare had spent the last few weeks in Hong Kong, and it was wonderful to be able to breathe freely without inhaling a mixture of cooking smells, body odours, and petrol fumes.

She returned her empty mug to the kitchen, and set off for the woods. It was another trip down memory lane as she started along the tree-lined path. Amazingly she remembered the way and found the spot she was looking for. The clearing was exactly as she had always seen it in her mind's eye. The stone fire pit was still there but it didn't look like there had been a fire in it for a long time.

Clare sat down on the log, the same place she'd sat with Wil all that time ago. She hugged herself and closed her eyes. Had it been a mistake to come back here? Surrounded by memories?

None of those memories had taken place here, though.

...Getting the part, a dream role, playing the kick-ass baddie, Shay Finch, was the high point of her life up until then. The Amy Ransom books were the first she'd read that helped her realise her feelings for women weren't some aberration exclusive to her. She'd had boyfriends in high school only because it was expected. But however hard Clare tried, she couldn't get past the kissing stage with any of the boys she had gone out with. They branded her a tease and called her all sorts of names, the kindest being "ice-queen." Crushes on teachers and older girls had all stayed in her head, unrealised fantasies.

Now she was actually going to meet the lesbian author who had helped her get through so many long nights. She had been overawed just meeting the actress who played the sexy sleuth, Amy Ransom. When Gemma Blake suggested she come along to help her give Kim a proper Aussie welcome on her arrival in the country, Clare had been too star-struck to say no.

Blake's idea of a welcome party involved an alcohol-fuelled boat ride around Sydney Harbour. After the tour, Blake abandoned her outside Kim's hotel with some lame excuse about leaving to work on her lines. The actress had never worked at anything in her life, but she had obviously engineered this meeting with meticulous planning. Blake had told Clare later that she knew she was gay from the moment she set eyes on her.

"How could you know that?"

"It's obvious, my dear. You don't flirt with any of the guys even though they're all ogling your tits and ass. You don't talk about anyone special in your life. And you look like you could do with a good shag."

"So you thought you would set me up with Kim Russell?"

"Sure. I know she likes blondes."

Maybe without Blake's intervention, it wouldn't have happened. Maybe she wouldn't have willingly followed Kim up to her hotel room…

Wrapped up in her thoughts, Clare didn't realise she was no longer alone until someone coughed. Looking up, she saw Sally gazing down at her, hands in pockets. Her hair was hidden under a ridiculous knitted bobble hat. Fashion sense aside, she was still an attractive woman.

"You looked miles away. Sorry to disturb you."

*You're not sorry, otherwise you would have walked on*, thought Clare. *And it was years, not miles.*

"Peaceful out here."

*It was.* Clare stood. "Getting cold, though. Better move on."

"Mind if I walk with you."

"Guess not." *Free country, and all.*

They set off down the path, walking side by side.

"So, what were you thinking about?"

*Wouldn't you like to know?* Clare looked up at the bare branches of the trees. "Another time, another country."

†

JJ had dismissed any thoughts that Shelley might have relaxed enough into their surroundings to welcome her embrace when she got into bed. She found that her partner had rolled over to one side and was pretending to be asleep. JJ could tell by her breathing that it was a sham. The last five minutes of preparation in the bathroom had been a waste of time.

With the early morning light filtering through the curtains, JJ could just make out the shape of Shelley's body on the far side of the bed, sleeping soundly now. Her own sleep had been fitful and she'd been kept awake going over things in her mind. Things she could do nothing about, but the thoughts kept going around, like a song you didn't want to hear stuck on a repeat cycle.

Would it have been a better start to the holiday if they had driven down? They had decided to take the train since the roads would be busy and the weather unpredictable. JJ was wishing now that they had brought her van, even though it wasn't the most comfortable of vehicles for long trips. Unfortunately, the train journey had proved to be a nightmare. Maybe it would be worth hiring a car to drive back.

She glanced over at her lover's bare shoulder and wondered how she was going to fix things between them. After five years of what she thought had been the best years of her life, Shelley had suddenly turned into a stranger. What had changed? JJ hadn't, that was for sure. Life was good now. They both had jobs they enjoyed or, at least, she thought they did. The irrepressible Candice had asked them what they did during dinner. JJ had told her about her painting and decorating business that was doing well. She'd answered for Shelley who was examining the food on her plate with forensic intensity.

"Shel's in real estate."

"That's nice," Candice offered, politely, but Shelley didn't look up to provide any more information. Sally, the other person determined to keep the conversation going at the table, had commented on the expected downturn in the housing market in London. She wondered if it was the same up north. Shelley didn't respond and Candice changed direction by asking Sally where she lived in London.

The evening had been pleasant enough, JJ thought, but more subdued than she had expected. The other guests seemed okay, although the Australian woman hadn't been happy with Candice's persistent attention. There would be more people around today, so that might help liven things up a bit. And there was some sort of entertainment planned with the evening meal

What were they going to do today? Going for a swim would only take up half an hour. Another reason they should have brought the van. At least they could have gone for a drive, maybe down to the coast. A walk in the woods would fill another half hour or so. She had noticed some board games on the bookcase in the lounge. But the last time she'd played Scrabble with Shelley they'd had a massive row, and the tiles ended up all over the floor. In her current mood Shelley certainly wasn't likely to want to play any games.

Well, breakfast first. A good start to the day might be to bring Shelley breakfast in bed. Store up some brownie points.

†

Pleased to find she hadn't lost her riding skills, Candice was enjoying the ride through the trails. They were going at a walking pace, as this was a first for Mags. The scenery surrounding them was lovely—very English countryside, a far cry from her native British Columbia forests.

The main reason for the trip had been to give Candice a chance to find out more about her ancestors. Filling out the gaps in her family tree had become something of an obsession. When she started the previous year, she had only expected to spend a few months on the project, seeing what she could find out from surviving elderly relatives and Internet sources. She hadn't thought her surname was so popular or could have so many variations. So many in the Irish diaspora that spread across North America had left only sporadic records. Hennessy was a much commoner name than she'd expected, and so far she hadn't found a connection with the founder of the well-known Cognac.

Perhaps her partner's moody disposition lately was exacerbated by following her around numerous graveyards and waiting while she trawled through parish records. Overall it hadn't netted much in the way of results. She had tried to interest Marguerite in tracing her own family tree. Mags hadn't thought it was worth the effort and Candice failed to convince her that finding out new things about her family and discovering lost connections was fascinating. Mags had just shrugged and said she wasn't interested in finding out she was descended from peasant farmers in the twelfth century. Bouchard was a common French name and the only thing she knew about it wasn't something she wanted to explore.

Wil Tyler led them along the trail through the woods that eventually opened out to a wide sloping meadow with a stream at the bottom. She stopped her silver mare and turned in the saddle, waiting for the others to reach her.

"That's the origin of the house name," she said, pointing downhill. "It only has water in it during the winter, and sometimes during a wet summer."

"I thought all summers were wet here." The unexpected comment came from Mags. She really had perked up.

"Not always, although having two or three sunny days in a row causes the water companies to panic and start talking about drought."

"You wouldn't think you'd have to worry about water supplies. This is only a small island."

"True. But we don't seem to be very good at managing it." Wil glanced at her watch. "I guess we should be heading back." She looked over at Mags. "Do you feel up to trying a faster pace, maybe a trot?"

Candice was surprised when Mags nodded enthusiastically.

"Okay. Just watch me and Candice. You'll soon get the hang of it. Shadow's used to novice riders so he won't give you any trouble. And give us a shout if you want to slow down again."

The journey back to the stables didn't take long and Mags actually seemed to be enjoying herself. When they got back, after thanking Wil and the horses, Candice suggested they go for a swim before lunch and was pleased when Mags agreed. Maybe all she had needed was a bit of fresh air and exercise to improve her mood.

†

Perching her six-foot frame on the edge of the stool wasn't comfortable, but it gave Ade a good view of her surroundings. The pub had changed dramatically from her first visit, twenty years or more earlier.

...Her relationship with Rita had been very new and maybe she had been trying to impress her with a trip to the countryside. However, it almost backfired. Doubling the lesbian population of the village was one thing, but Ade was sure they were the only black people any of the inhabitants had seen in the flesh. When people asked her where she was from, she told them Scotland. Anyone wanted her to go back to her country of origin, that's where she would be heading.

Kim had warned them that, as well as serving a lacklustre selection of beers, the pub wasn't likely to be a welcoming place. When Kim arrived back from the race meeting she'd gone to for the day, both Ade and Rita were a bit on the tipsy side. Deciding to ignore the overtly hostile looks directed their way to have more than one drink—they had, at least, provided some entertainment for the uptight band of locals.

That had been a weekend to remember in more ways than one. It was the first time Kim and Grace slept together. But Grace wasn't the only unexpected visitor. Wil had turned up the next morning after running away from the foster home she'd been placed in after her mother's untimely death. Ade never got the full story from either Kim or Wil, but it had been the start of something new for both of them...

Mark placed a pint of bitter in front of her; something called Sheep Shanks that he assured her was the best of their beers on tap despite the name. Toby waved to her on his way through to the kitchen. They had a chef but Toby was in charge of the catering side of their business. Ade seemed to remember the old Good Shepherd's only contribution to food had been a jar of pickled eggs on the counter, which had looked like a science experiment gone wrong, and packets of pork scratchings. Toby had elevated their output to a gourmet level with sandwiches any London deli would be proud to serve and a tempting selection of three-course meals in the evening.

"Is Rita joining you?" Mark asked, wiping the counter in front of her.

"No. She's got the bit between her teeth. Trying to get Gaby to slow down and take it easy."

"I'd like to see how that works out."

"I don't think Gaby stands a chance. Anyway, are you okay with loaning Toby out for this evening?"

"Yep, it's all good. Sandy's mum is coming in for a few hours to help cover the bar."

"Great. We appreciate it. The kids need a break."

He smiled. "We've been trying to tell Gaby..." His next words were cut short as two more customers arrived.

Ade turned her head to check out the newcomers. The two women looked so out of place that they had to be guests at the house. Remembering Clare's nicknames from the night before, she reckoned they had to be the ones she'd called Sulky Shelley and Jumping Jane, aka JJ. They placed their order and went over to sit at a corner table near the fire. The sulky one immediately got out her phone and stared at the screen intently, then got up abruptly and came over to the bar. Mark had just finished pouring a glass of white wine and was topping up the pint of beer from the tap.

"What's the Wi-Fi code?"

He pointed to the sign at the end of the bar. It gave details for guest logins.

"Oh, thanks. At least you've got a decent signal here. I haven't been able to get anything up at the house."

"Yeah, it's a bit hit and miss there."

Ade watched the woman walk back to her table, trying to place the accent. Somewhere up north, Manchester possibly. It wasn't Liverpudlian anyway. Mark carried their drinks over, and then went to stoke up the fire.

"Ha! I thought I'd find you here." Wil pulled up the stool next to her and hopped onto it with an agility Ade could only envy.

"Really. I only said I was going for a walk."

"I know your walks. They don't usually involve wandering through nature trails."

"What are you doing here, anyway? I thought you were incredibly busy today."

"This is one of my jobs. I'm driving Mark back, along with some food supplies. Just a half of that Sheep Shit, thanks."

Mark had returned to the bar and got a glass down from the shelf above his head. "I wish you wouldn't call it that in front of customers."

"What customers? We don't count."

He nodded towards the fireplace. "Some of yours, I believe. Already complaining about the lousy phone signal at your place."

Wil glanced around and noticed the couple in the corner. "Oh, yeah. Well, it's all part of the package. It's meant to be a retreat. Get away from the distractions of the outside world."

"And it stops them from cheating when you give them the Christmas Quiz."

"Someone always finds a way. Do you remember that woman who was so desperate to win, she climbed out onto the roof?"

Ade laughed. "Who could forget? Made everyone's day when the fire brigade turned up and two of the firefighters were women."

"Yeah, after that I thought we were going to have a spate of false alarms." Wil drank most of her half pint in one long gulp. She looked over at Mark. "Is the stuff ready? We should probably get back. It's almost lunchtime."

"I'll go check."

"Okay. We'll meet you at the car." She looked at Ade's glass, still half full. "Drink up, mate. We've got work to do."

As if on cue, Ade's phone rang. She pulled it out of her pocket and winced when she saw Rita's face on the screen. "Hi, Hon. Yes, all in hand. Just helping Wil with the food order." She ended the call. "I swear she's psychic."

"No. She just knows all your bad habits." Wil finished her drink and slid off the stool. She went over to the couple in the corner and Ade heard her offer to give them a lift back to the house. Luckily they turned her down. It would have been a bit of a squeeze in the confines of the Subaru.

†

Walking with Clare was a silent business. Concentrating on the path and trying to keep up with the actress's long-legged stride, Sally tried to think of ways to draw her out. Maybe she shouldn't have interrupted her reverie. Obviously there were some long-held memories here. Memories she wanted to winkle out.

"So, I gather you've been here before," she ventured. A substitute for *do you come here often?*—not her chat up line of choice.

"Once. A long time ago."

"Has it changed much?"

"Well, the inside of the house has mostly been refurbished. And the swimming pool wasn't here."

"The place you were sitting. Was that a special place for you?"

Clare slowed her pace and looked down at her. *Gorgeous blue eyes,* Sally thought. She could get lost in there. And the hair. She could almost feel the silky strands slipping through her fingers as they kissed.

"What are you after, Sally?" The roughness of Clare's tone shook her out of her daydream.

"Nothing. Just making conversation." Sally spread her hands, the universal gesture showing she had nothing to hide. The blue eyes seemed to peer through her, probing her mind for the truth.

"Really. You just happened to be out for a walk and stumbled across me. In what? A hundred and fifty acres?" Clare came to a standstill.

Sally just stopped short of bumping into her. They were, she realised, at a fork in the path.

"If you go down there," Clare said, pointing to the left hand option, "it will take you in a circular route back to the house. I'm going to walk this way. And I want to be alone." She stalked off down the other trail.

*You and Greta Garbo,* thought Sally. What was it with actresses? She hadn't thought Clare was the prima donna type. Well, she hadn't been left with much choice. She could hardly run after her. Still there were other avenues to pursue. Perhaps a trip to the stables was in order.

†

Wil set the last of the boxes on the counter by the door and looked over at Gaby. Her long black hair was tied back but a few strands had escaped and fell across her eyes as she bent over her task. She was seated at the table putting the finishing touches on a tray of small savoury pastries.

If she could have been sure of a warm welcome, Wil would have gone over and moved the hair out of her lover's eyes before lowering her head for a kiss. And up until a few weeks ago, she would have been sure of the kiss being accepted and returned with Gaby's usual fervour.

She was certain Gaby knew she was there, but was keeping her head down, another deliberate avoidance tactic. Wil stumbled out onto the patio, her eyes suddenly wet. Setting off across the lawn at a run, she soon found herself on a familiar trail. She slowed down and forced herself to keep breathing.

Relieved to find the clearing empty, Wil sat on the log by the fire pit and rested her head in her hands. Many times she had come here with Kim, particularly in the months before her death, when she couldn't walk far without being out of breath. Wil could recall their last serious conversation on a bright autumn day just before she left for her trip to Rome.

...She arrived at the house to pick up a few things she needed and was dismayed to find Kim slumped on the floor in the study with an empty bottle of Glenfiddich at her feet. It wasn't an unusual sight, and one that had become more frequent. With difficulty she managed to rouse Kim and get some coffee into her along with a few rounds of toast. They had gone for a walk, taking it slowly as Kim's movements had the lethargy of someone wading through deep slushy snow.

It was up to Wil to keep a conversation going. She talked about the work she was doing for her master's degree. After finishing with a first in her BA Honours degree in linguistics from UCL, she was continuing with more research on the Etruscan language. The subject fascinated her but she realised by the time they reached the pond at the edge of the woods that she'd lost Kim some time before.

"That's great," Kim said, when she stopped for breath. "But who are you screwing?"

Wil winced. It was almost word for word the same question Ade had asked her the week before. "No one special at the moment," she said, repeating her reply to Ade.

"But you do have a sex life, I hope."

"Sometimes. It's just a distraction, though. I'm not ready for any long-term relationships."

Kim gave a snort of something that might have been an attempt at laughter. "You mean you don't want to follow my example. Sorry I'm such a shit role model."

"It's not that. I just haven't met anyone I like that much."

"What about the Chinese girl you brought down at Christmas?"

"Lin? Yeah, well she was sweet, but it was never going to last. She was just experimenting. I think she really just wanted to know if my pubes were the same colour as the hair on my head."

Kim really did laugh then. They had reached the clearing and sat down opposite each other on the logs. Kim picked up a stick and poked at the ground between her feet.

"I want you to find someone who'll love you."

They'd had this conversation before and it disturbed Wil. She loved Kim and worried about her constantly, especially when she saw her looking as frail as she did now. Grace's visits always left Kim in an unbalanced state of mind. She had recognised Grace's lingering scent in the hallway when she'd arrived that morning. She went over to Kim and sat next to her.

"I will find someone. But I'm only twenty-one for fuck's sake."...

She had found someone in Rome, and Gaby, far from being a momentary distraction, turned out to be her lifesaver. Wil really hadn't thought she would ever fall in love so completely. To lose Gaby was unthinkable. She couldn't help it as a sob escaped. This just couldn't be happening now.

† 

The path Clare had chosen brought her out at the pond, and with a sense of relief at having shaken off the other woman, she made her way back down the trail leading to the clearing. It had been peaceful there and she wanted to continue, as she had told Sally, to be alone with her thoughts.

Why hadn't she pursued the relationship with Kim? They had been good together. Maybe it was because their encounters had something of the holiday romance about them. Kim was only ever visiting. And when she was filming, she was emotionally on edge all the time. Did Kim just happen to turn up when Clare was playing a part, the sexy villain? The woman the fans loved to hate. It had been a fun part to play. And her time with Kim was characterised by lightheartedness, a two-month long romp on the beach.

Had she sensed the writer had unresolved issues? Kim had packed up quickly and left when Wil called her. Clare had been planning to introduce Kim to her family. Something she'd never done before. Then suddenly Kim was gone, back to her real life. The hurt had stayed with Clare for a long time, the feeling of rejection. But when they met up again at a film premiere in San Francisco, it was as if the intervening months had never happened.

The clearing wasn't empty when Clare returned but she swallowed her disappointment quickly when she saw the figure huddled there. She sat down on the log opposite, the fire pit providing a space between them. As had happened with her own meditations earlier Clare wasn't sure if her presence would be welcomed.

Wil looked up and Clare could see she'd been crying. She had sensed the night before that Wil had been waiting for Ade to show up and she had left them alone so they could talk. It looked like the problem was still unresolved.

"Do you want to talk about it," Clare asked, gently.

"Nothing much to say. Gaby thinks I'm having an affair."

Clare resisted asking, *and are you?* She was sure Wil wouldn't be short on offers. But she also knew from her previous visit how much in love the young couple were. And it was hard to believe anything had changed. They seemed so well suited to each other.

"Anyway, Rita's set it up so we can have dinner together tonight. But, in the kitchen just now, Gaby wouldn't even look at me. How can she think I would cheat on her?"

"Well, I've never been pregnant, but I understand it can do funny things to the mind. Paranoia is probably high on the list."

"I just wouldn't. She's my life."

Clare was at a loss. She had never felt that way about anyone. Kim Russell had been the closest she'd come to feeling something other than short-lived bursts of lust with anyone.

"What are you going to do to convince her?" she asked.

"I don't know. Ade's getting some flowers for tonight."

"Oh, no. She really will think you're having an affair if you present her with flowers. Been there, could write the script. Is there something else you can give her? What have you got her for Christmas?"

Wil looked at her then, eyes widening. "Shit! Of course. Thank you, Clare." She jumped up and raced out of the clearing.

Clare stood and moved her legs, feeling the cold seeping into her bones. With slow, deliberate movements, she started the sequence of patterns that were ingrained in her muscle memory. When she returned to her real life in Sydney, she would be taking her third Dan Taekwondo grading, and she had promised her instructor she would practice the *Poomsae* moves every day. Starting with the first pattern she had learned to gain her yellow belt at the age of eight, she warmed up through the ten forms that preceded the one she needed to know for her grading: *Taebaek*, supreme brightness. As well as perfecting her tiger stance, she was working on the new movements in this pattern, the small hinge block and the double knife-hand low-section block. Hinge blocks weren't a favourite, but knife-hands she liked.

After a third run through of *Taebaek*, Clare was dripping with sweat. A cool off in the pool beckoned and she was fairly certain she would have it to herself.

†

The path did indeed lead eventually to the lawn at the back of the house. Feeling she'd had enough of a nature walk for one day, Sally walked around the side of the building and onto the drive. Really, they should provide golf carts or something to give guests transport down to the stables. It was a bit of a hike. But, at least it was downhill. The lack of phone signals was puzzling as the house was located at the top of the hill. But she supposed the trees got in the way. It was something of a black spot for anyone wanting to be connected to the outside world via their digital devices. The Wi-Fi was so intermittent she thought she could file for false advertising.

The stable buildings came into view. Sally guessed the biggest one must be where the horses were and, as she got closer, the sounds of large animals moving around reached her ears, but not before the smell had already assaulted her nose.

Thelma had given her only a sketchy description of Felicity Evans. Apart from short grey hair, weather-beaten face, and bowlegs from years of riding, the other outstanding feature was apparently a finger missing on one hand. Resisting the idea of making a smart remark about sharp-hipped girls from Sheffield, Sally approached the figure working in the open stall. She had the short grey hair but

Sally couldn't tell about the number of fingers. The woman was wearing gloves and one hand gripped the knife she was using to open up a bale of what Sally supposed was straw. There was a wheelbarrow full of wet foul-smelling stuff by the door. Even though not given to reading horse sagas, Sally could venture an educated guess that the woman was engaged in the activity known as "mucking out."

"Hi," Sally said to signal her presence, although she was sure her approach had already been noted.

The woman looked up and tucked the knife into the sheath on her belt. Her lined face had the look of someone who'd spent a lifetime outdoors, but her stance wasn't particularly bowlegged.

When the other woman didn't speak, Sally continued, "I'm looking for Mrs Evans."

"Tack room," was all the answer she got before the woman continued with her task and started spreading the straw around the stall.

"Right, thanks." Sally went back outside and took in a lungful of fresher air, although it still smelled strongly of horse. *What the fuck is a tack room?* Looking around she saw a shed-like structure at the end of the stable block. She approached cautiously, hoping that the elusive Mrs Evans was a bit more clued up about customer relations.

As she reached the door she could hear voices. This morning was turning out to be a dud. Sally really needed to talk to the old woman on her own. Pushing open the door, she walked into a fug of smoke. A man was seated astride one of the saddles on the stands that were lined alongside one wall. Sally guessed that he'd said goodbye to fifty a long time ago, but he still had a good head of hair, white with touches of black clinging on. The process of elimination was fairly simple. He had to be the father of the mysterious Gabriella she had seen briefly the day before. He was puffing on a small brown cigarillo that she recognised from a short fling she'd had with the same brand during her university days.

His companion was a much older woman who was rubbing at a piece of leather, a cigarette hanging out of one side of her mouth. They stopped talking when she came in and looked at her warily. Her interruption obviously wasn't welcome.

"Um. Sorry. I was looking for Wil."

"She went out with two other guests a while ago. Should be back by lunchtime."

Sally could see the hand with an index finger missing as the woman removed the cigarette from her mouth to answer. Well, now she knew what Mrs Evans looked like. Although if she'd seen Felicity and Rose side by side she would have had difficulty telling them apart. Felicity Evans looked like she would be a hard nut to crack, not particularly friendly. She would have to try to talk to her another time. Nodding slowly, Sally backed out and closed the door. This was a dead end, for now anyway.

She stood in the yard and considered her next move. It was a toss up between Ade McPherson and Wil Tyler. Both were key to the story she wanted to tell. The old woman, Thelma Barton, had warned her to tread carefully in her approach to Wil in particular, making her sound like a wild creature that required patient tracking and stalking. Well, not stalking, in the current sense.

Wilma Talbot, as she had once been. The story of her mother's untimely death hadn't been hard to unravel, even from the sketchy newspaper reports from twenty-two years earlier. It had hit the headlines briefly when the connection was made with Kim Russell, the reclusive lesbian author. But she had never been implicated in her lover's death. The circumstances were far removed from the picturesque Sussex countryside where Kim was recovering from wounds sustained in a near fatal car crash. That was another story Sally meant to ferret out.

There had been no mention of the daughter in any reports she'd read. Thelma had only hinted at the kind of childhood Wil would have had. Sally could piece it together. Wil and her mother had moved constantly, one step ahead of the bailiffs. Sally imagined the loneliness of the child reaching her teenage years, never staying in one place long enough to form long-lasting friendships. Always the outsider, always the loner. Always something to hide. Little wonder she had changed her surname as soon as she was able to.

From what she had seen of Wil so far, Sally could sense a lingering tightness, a controlled nature. It wasn't something you would get over completely, Sally thought, your mother brutally murdered. The detritus of her life exposed in national news. Luckily it was long before the advent of social media outlets. Still there would be lasting scars. Much as she hated to admit it, Thelma had been right. Sally would need to tread carefully.

†

Wil wondered for the umpteenth time that day why she had agreed to this date idea. It was obvious Gaby didn't want to speak to her, so she wasn't likely to want to sit at the table and share a meal with her. When was the last time they had done that? It was probably that fateful day in March when they had come up with the idea of asking Mark if he would be the sperm donor for their child. It wasn't a new idea. Gaby had been talking about wanting a child before she reached forty for some time. He had been delighted to be asked. They had been warned that it might not take first time. But it had. And before they knew it they were on their way to new parenthood.

There weren't any prenatal classes nearby, but Emily Harris on the neighbouring farm was a trained midwife. Emily had talked them through the important bits and promised to be on hand when the baby came. Gaby's long Skype sessions with her mother also provided her with more first-hand information, including detailed descriptions of the birth of each of her siblings. Gaby seemed calm about the whole thing, but Wil was getting more nervous about what could go wrong as the time for the birth drew nearer. Just because Gaby hadn't had any health issues during the pregnancy so far didn't mean it couldn't still happen. There was still time for disaster to strike. Wil stopped reading the graphic descriptions in the books they now had in abundance.

Having acted on Clare's jolt to her memory, Wil busied herself with the routine jobs that needed doing in an effort to keep her mind off the evening encounter to come. The rooms with fireplaces were now stocked with enough wood to last through the next few days. She'd brought up all the wine from the cellar that would be required for the evening meal and the next day. Mulled wine had been put out for the guests and she had refilled the jug several times. From what she could see, Shelley seemed to be drinking it as if it were orange juice. She was going to have one hell of a hangover if she didn't slow down. But it wasn't Wil's business to tell the guests not to drink themselves into oblivion if that's what they wanted to do. She wasn't sure why the couple from Manchester had booked to stay with them. They hadn't shown an interest in any of the activities on offer. Apart from the trip to pub, they didn't seem to have moved from the lounge. JJ was leafing through a magazine while her partner was mainly fiddling with her phone.

Ade found Wil checking the table settings in the dining room just before seven.

"What do you think you're doing?"

"The table doesn't set itself." Wil realigned one of the Christmas crackers.

"Well, it looks great. Time for you to go upstairs. You might want to get changed."

Wil looked down at her attire. She was wearing a pair of loose fitting jeans and a Christmas jumper with a large image of a reindeer on it. "What's wrong with this?"

"About as sexy as…"

"We won't be having sex, even if she does deign to speak to me."

"You could make the effort, though. For Rita's sake, at least. She's invested a lot of thought and energy into this reconciliation."

Now, standing in front of the wardrobe, Wil pulled out the dark green shirt Gaby had bought for her the previous year. She'd said it complemented Wil's hair colour and her eyes, but Wil thought it made her look like a Christmas elf. Still, she'd have put on the full costume, including pointy ears, if there were any chance it would help.

The table in their kitchenette was set for two and the settings looked similar to the ones in the dining room downstairs. She'd brought up two crackers but although the colourfully wrapped tubes added a festive touch, Wil wasn't sure Gaby would be in the mood to share in the joy of pulling them apart.

After Clare had dissuaded her from the flower bouquet idea she had arranged them in several vases and placed them around the lounge. She'd overheard Candice enthusing about how nice it was to have fresh cut flowers in the house in December instead of the usual over abundance of poinsettias. Candice was easily pleased, she thought. But at least the Canadian couple was looking cheerful. Marguerite had certainly perked up since the day before and Wil had observed them in a mushy embrace behind the Christmas tree in the hall on her way back from one of her cellar trips with the wine.

She poured out two glasses of water. A taste of the red wine breathing on the counter would have been more useful in settling her nerves, but Gaby was taking care not to drink alcohol during her pregnancy and Wil usually succeeded in being supportive by not drinking in her presence. She corked the wine bottle and moved it out of sight. She was sure Ade wouldn't let it go to waste.

Seven-thirty. Show time. Rita had promised to make sure Gaby relinquished her kitchen duties for the evening. And sure enough, Wil could hear footsteps on the stairs. The slow measured steps Gaby was taking nowadays. Until the sixth month no one would have known she was pregnant, the bump hardly showing with her stylish, loose tops. Now it looked like she was carrying twins. Wil didn't know how her slim frame supported the weight. In spite of the lessons, she still found the whole process baffling.

As the footsteps drew closer, Wil bit her lip and wiped her hands on her jeans again. She hadn't felt this nervous since that first night they'd made love.

Gaby stopped in the doorway to catch her breath. Her natural beauty was as heart stopping as usual, but Wil could see the exhaustion in her eyes. Those lovely dark eyes looked past her at the elaborately set table, then back to her.

"Is this really supposed to make up for you cheating on me?" she said, sadly.

"I haven't…"

"Don't even try to deny it. All those afternoons you've been sneaking down to the village. Did you think I hadn't noticed?"

"Gaby!"

"If it's over, I thought you would at least have the guts to tell me." She turned away and started to move towards their bedroom.

"Gaby! This is ridiculous. Do you want to see what I've been doing in the village?"

"What? Have you brought her here?"

Wil shook her head. She had to do something. "Come on. In the nursery." She walked past Gaby down the short hallway. The nursery was opposite their bedroom. She opened the door and waited. Gaby's curiosity got the better of her and sure enough she followed Wil in.

"Let me introduce you to my mistress."

The handcrafted cradle was in the centre of the room where Mark had placed it earlier in the day. She had called him after Clare's timely reminder in the woods, and she had needed his help to carry it up the stairs.

Gaby went over to the cradle and sank to her knees. She stroked the wood and set it rocking. Finally she looked up at Wil, tears streaming. "You made this?"

Wil sat down next to her. "Yes. Mark got the wood, but I carved the runners and put it together. I was just waiting for the last coat of varnish to dry before bringing it here. It was meant to be a Christmas surprise."

"Wil," she sniffed. "I'm so sorry."

"I thought, you know, the first little while, we'll want the baby with us at night. And…"

"Oh, Wil," Gaby pulled her closer. It was an awkward position but somehow they managed to find each other's lips and kiss. In spite of the discomfort, Wil would have been happy to stay there for an eternity.

When they broke apart, she smiled at Gaby. "We'd better go and eat that food. Rita will kill us if we don't."

Gaby's answering smile deepened the dimples on her cheeks. "You'll have to help me up, *cara*."

"*Con piacere.*"

She gave a mock groan as she helped Gaby to her feet. "Are you sure it's not twins?"

Gaby shook her head. She looked down at the cradle. "Could we eat in here? I don't want to leave. I just want to gaze at this now."

"Of course, that's a brilliant idea."

Wil gathered the duvet and pillows from their bed and got Gaby settled on the sofa. She returned with the dish of braised lamb, putting the vegetables in as well. It would be easier for them both to eat out of the one container rather than bothering with plates.

†

Candice hadn't really expected a gourmet dinner on Christmas Eve. Booking at a lesbian-run guesthouse had seemed like a different idea for Christmas even if it meant having nut roast instead of turkey for the main event. Seven courses, though. This was amazing. It put their last Christmas meal at the Four Seasons Hotel in Vancouver in the shade. Who would have thought that you could have fine dining in this backwater in rural England?

She glanced across the table at Mags and was pleased to see her engaging Clare in conversation. Her partner was more successful than she had been in drawing the reluctant actress out of her shell. It seemed Clare was familiar with the ski resorts of Whistler and Banff, and they were discussing the merits of each with some vigour. Sally, seated next to her, was hanging onto every word, but Candice thought she was just waiting for a chance to butt in. Full of questions, that one. When asked about herself, she always deflected with another query.

"More *vino tinto, signora?*"

Candice looked up at the man and nodded. Gabriella's father was certainly enjoying himself, serving the wine with great aplomb, dressed in black trousers, white shirt, and sporting a bow tie that flashed on and off. He had shared a cracker with the woman from the stables and was now also wearing a red party hat. The tall black woman who had introduced herself as Ade had joined them for dinner, along with an older woman, Rose. It seemed they had been allocated the hosting role for the evening and sat at either ends of the table. Their respective partners, Rita and Felicity, were helping with the production and serving of the meal. Candice thought Ade's elegant partner, Rita, was better suited to waitressing as the horsewoman just looked like a comedy actress playing a role. She suspected the horses were given more friendly looks when they were fed.

"What do you do, Candice?"

She turned her head. Ade was looking at her expectantly.

"I design and develop online learning materials."

"Oh, like, what are they are called now, MOOCs? Is that it?"

"Massive Open Online Courses. Yes, that's it. FutureLearn is the big player here as they develop courses for your Open University."

"I feel like I'm behind the times and I've only been retired a few years."

"Were you in computers?"

"Yes, programming."

Their discussion on the merits of Apple versus Samsung was interrupted when JJ insisted on silence while she read out the joke from her cracker.

"Okay, everyone. Can you guess the answer to this? How did Scrooge win the football game?"

With a collective groan, they all shook their heads.

"The ghost of Christmas passed."

More groans and a quick shuffle of hands digging the small slips of paper out from the rubble of the cracker debris left on the table.

Clare was the next to join in.

"Why did Santa's helper see the doctor?" She looked around the table. "No takers. Okay. Because he had low elf esteem."

Rose followed this. "What do you get if you cross a bell with a skunk?"

To Candice's amazement, Mags jumped in. "Oh, I know that one. Jingle smells."

They carried on around the table and only stopped when the next course was brought in.

"Was there going to be some entertainment this evening?" This came from Sally.

Candice remembered there had been something on the programme about a group of hand-bell ringers, whatever that was.

Ade answered. "Yes, but unfortunately they called to say they wouldn't make it. Apparently it's snowing in Hertfordshire. Not likely to reach us though."

"Where's Hertfordshire?" asked Shelley, the first words she'd spoken throughout the meal. She hadn't even joined in the joke reading.

"Just north of London."

"Oh, I thought it was near Wales."

"No, that's Hereford."

"Oh," Shelley subsided into silence again.

There was a general lack of conversation around the table as everyone started on the exquisitely presented plate of what had been described on the menu as ham hock croquettes with pickles, quail's egg, and pea puree. How did they think these things up, Candice wondered. It was a far cry from the lentil surprise she'd been expecting for every meal.

†

If that was the Christmas Eve dinner, JJ wasn't sure how they could possibly do better for the lunch on Christmas Day. Sitting in the lounge, fully stuffed, she couldn't imagine wanting to eat again for a very long time. There was coffee as well as a comprehensive range of after-dinner drinks on offer—port, scotch, cognac, and more sherry.

Shelley had barely spoken while they were eating. JJ had been uncomfortably aware of how it might look to the others and felt she had to do something to liven up the mood. Fortunately, everyone else had taken the cracker joke sharing in good spirits and joined in enthusiastically.

She wished Shelley would cheer up. Even Mags had gotten into the spirit of things and was now doing a slow dance with her partner while they waited for Ade to return with their drinks. Sally had seated herself next to Clare on the sofa even though it looked like the actress would have preferred for her to sit somewhere else.

If they were at home now, what would they be doing? After their first year together, they had avoided spending Christmas with either of their families. Last year they had shared a villa in Portugal with four of their friends. JJ had thought they might do that again this year, but Shelley had insisted she wanted to do something that didn't involve getting on a plane. JJ hadn't disagreed with that. Avoiding the crowded airports at peak holiday times was a good idea. They could take trips abroad during school term times when it wasn't so expensive and marginally less hectic.

Her reverie was disturbed when Shelley stood suddenly.

"Are you okay, hon?"

"Yeah. Just going to the loo."

Ade came in with the drinks as Shelley left the room. Setting the tray down carefully, Ade looked at JJ. "Is she all right?"

"Yes, thanks." JJ accepted the glass of brandy and thought, *no, she's not, but I don't know what to do about it.*

Candice and Mags rejoined the group and JJ sipped her drink quietly, listening to the others as they shared stories of childhood Christmases. They agreed with Ade and Sally that it was a shame that the original "Christmas Carol" film, starring Alistair Sim as Scrooge, was no longer shown on Christmas Eve.

JJ finished her brandy and said goodnight. "Better go and see if Shelley's okay. I thought she was coming right back. See you all in the morning."

With a chorus of goodnights and Merry Christmases ringing in her ears, she left the festive atmosphere of the lounge and trudged up the stairs, wondering what she was going to find.

She entered the room expecting to see Shelley in bed, but it was empty as was the bathroom. Shelley came in just as JJ was wondering where she could be. She looked flushed.

"I thought you must be in bed since you didn't come back."

Shelley shrugged. "I just needed some fresh air. And I really didn't want another drink."

"You're okay, aren't you?"

"Yeah, fine. I'm going to bed now, though." She pushed past JJ and closed the bathroom door in her face.

JJ sighed. This was going to be a long night. She went over to the window and gazed out. The two wire frame horses looked ghostly in the cold glare of the moonlit night. There was already a heavy frost on the ground. Ade had said she didn't think they would get any snow, but it seemed cold enough.

†

Escaping from Sally's clutches once again, Clare grabbed her coat from the hall cupboard and opened the front door. She stood in the drive and looked up at the stars. So clear, so bright. She was reminded of summer nights in the desert, waiting for the darkness to experience the closeness of the galaxies; to feel a connection with those far away worlds.

"Amazing! I don't think I've ever seen so many stars. They look close enough to reach out and touch."

Clare hadn't heard Sally come out and looked over at the other woman with some dismay, wondering what she had to do to shake off her attention. She had deliberately seated herself between Marguerite and JJ at dinner, and realised her mistake when the only seat left was the one opposite. Fortunately, the formerly incommunicative Mags was giving the impression of an outgoing individual and kept the Londoner's imminent inquisition at bay.

Clare thought about turning back into the house, but on reflection she realised it was selfish not to share the beauty of the night. No point in spoiling either of their evenings by being rude.

"I hardly ever notice the stars. Too much light pollution where I live."

"And where do you live, Sally?"

"Hackney. Or I should say, East Highbury. Sounds more upmarket."

"I don't know London very well. Only the bit around the theatre district."

"Ah, well. You need to expand your horizons."

They both stood looking up at the sky.

"Look, I'm sorry about earlier. Coming back here has triggered a few memories." For some reason Clare felt she needed to apologise for her brusqueness in the woods.

"Well, I guess I shouldn't have disturbed you. Look, I'm getting a bit chilled. How would you like a nightcap? I've got some Bushmills in my room."

Clare breathed out slowly. "Yeah, sure. Sounds good."

†

Ade finished the downstairs fire checks and found Rita in the dining room putting out the candles.

"That went well," she said without looking round.

"Yep. Thanks to you."

"I did have help. Teresa and Guido were star performers. I think they really enjoyed themselves. Guido says he likes English Christmas traditions. He's probably gone to bed in his party hat."

"Yeah, and he insisted on collecting everyone's cracker jokes." Ade laughed and moved in close. "Do you think it's safe to go up, now? Will the kids be in bed?"

"I certainly hope so. If not, I'll knock both their heads together into next week." Rita smiled at Ade, the mischief in her eyes belying her stern tone. She placed her hands on Ade's waist and shimmied her hips against her. "Now, I seem to remember you were promising me some action last night."

"Only if you've been good. Santa's little helper won't be coming out to play if you haven't."

Rita gave her another teasing smile. "Oh, I've been good. You wouldn't believe how good I've been." Her hands had travelled down and grasped Ade's butt.

"Sure you're not too tired? You've had a busy day." Rita's expert touch was sending shivers up her spine, not to mention the moistness developing in her groin.

"You're not chickening out on me, are you, McPherson?"

"Not on your life. But I think we should take this upstairs. We don't want Gaby's parents walking in on us while I ravage you on the table."

They made it upstairs with their clothes on, just.

# Chapter Three

## Christmas Morning

Waking up on Christmas morning, Ade looked over at Rita's sleeping form, and gave thanks again for whatever divine being had been looking out for her by bringing them together. Having watched so many of her friends settle into what looked like dull domesticity, she hadn't expected to fall in love. Approaching forty, she had thought love had passed her by and she was forever doomed to be the ageing singleton invited to make up the numbers at Christmas and other family-oriented occasions.

Rita had taken her in hand from their very first date. She insisted Ade court her. It had been six long weeks before she permitted more than a kiss. The whole thing made Ade feel about fifteen again, wanting something so badly, something that was always just out of reach. But she enjoyed it. Enjoyed Rita's teasing glances and hints. Rita made her work for what she wanted but when she got it, for once in her life Ade wasn't disappointed. And it had been her mission, for the last twenty years, to make sure she lived up to Rita's expectations.

One of those was their Christmas morning tradition. Champagne and stockings by the fire. She got up and managed to wash and dress without waking her lover.

The small sitting room was cold but she soon had the fire going. She placed Rita's stocking next to the one already leaning against the chimney breast. The mini fir tree in the corner was doing duty as the present magnet. There was a pile of neatly wrapped gifts already under it. Those would be the ones from Gaby. Anything from Wil would be covered in old newspaper or tinfoil she'd raided from the kitchen.

Ade took the champagne out of the fridge and collected four glasses. Before going in to wake Rita she thought she should check on the children. To her surprise, and initial alarm, their bed was empty. Then she noticed the duvet and pillows were missing. Following her instinct she looked in the nursery. They looked like two babes in the wood, snuggled into the duvet, the remains of the evening meal on the floor next to them.

Rita was in the kitchenette when she got back, drinking a glass of orange juice.

"Merry Christmas, sweetheart. You have to come and see this. It's too cute."

"Merry Christmas to you, too. What is it?"

Ade took her hand and led her down the hall to the nursery. When they reached the doorway, she held her finger to her lips. Rita peeked in and Ade could feel her whole body shaking with silent laughter.

†

Another Christmas Day waking up in a strange room, in another country, a long way from home—and alone. Clare had been tempted the night before, after a few whiskies with Sally in her room, the bed only feet away. But she hadn't crossed that line.

They exchanged stories, sharing laughter. She sensed Sally wanted more from her. But more, what? She'd answered Candice's questions at the dinner table about the Shay Finch TV series that was under discussion. When Sally started to ask her what it had been like meeting the author, she deflected the question and told her some stories about working with Gemma Blake. It was safer ground than taking another trip down that other memory lane.

The quietness of the morning was taking root. It was always quiet here, apart from a few creaking floorboards and the sound of the central heating system coming on; a gurgling in the radiators that probably hadn't been bled since the year before. No birds tweeting.

Finally Clare got up and padded over to the window. Pulling back the curtain, her eyes were dazzled by the view. A blanket of white covered everything and snow was still falling. Suddenly the feeling of loneliness she had awakened with disappeared. This in itself was worth the trip. A snowy wonderland on Christmas Day. It was all her childhood fantasies come true. A white Christmas.

† 

JJ passed Candice on the stairs. She was carrying a tray filled with breakfast goodies that included coffee, orange juice, croissants, and a pile of crispy bacon.

"A little Christmas feast for my sweetie."

"Well, um, Merry Christmas to you both."

*Lucky old Mags,* thought JJ. It had been a shock waking to find an empty bed, but then she thought maybe Shelley was going to surprise her by bringing breakfast up. It had never happened before, but there was always a first time. Perhaps Shelley wanted to make up for being a moody cow for the last few days.

There was a light snow falling. She had thought it was even quieter than usual when she woke. First, no Shelley in the bed or the bathroom, then the snow covering the ground outside, the dark tree trunks standing out in stark relief against the layer of whiteness. JJ decided the breakfast wasn't on its way and that maybe Shelley had gone out to enjoy the winter wonderland. She washed and dressed quickly and went downstairs.

The kitchen was silent as well. There was still coffee in the pot though. It was hot and fresh. She added milk and sugar and opened the back door to watch the snow. Holding the mug close to her chest she breathed in the fresh air. More snow was building up on the ground and the lawn was a sea of white. There were no footprints, so Shelley couldn't have gone out that way. Still holding the coffee, JJ closed the door and walked back down the hallway to the front of the house. The tree lights were off so it seemed none of the hosts were up yet, even though it was after nine o'clock. Christmas morning. The guests had been told to amuse themselves until the festivities started at eleven.

JJ peered into the lounge. No one there either. She looked out of the window that faced the drive. No prints or tracks of any kind could be seen in the pristine whiteness everywhere.

Surely Shelley couldn't have gone out in this. JJ put her mug down on the table and raced out to the hall cupboard. They'd left their winter jackets there the day before after coming back from the pub. She rooted through the jumble frantically. Shelley's coat wasn't there. She checked again. This was mad.

Opening the front door, a gust of snow blew into her face. She shut it again quickly.

†

Wil struggled to her feet. She couldn't believe they'd fallen asleep on the sofa. Gaby looked so peaceful. She decided to let her slumber on. Time for a quick shower and change before starting the day. It had been a long time since she'd slept in her clothes and she didn't like the feeling, or the smell.

There were signs in the kitchenette that Ade and Rita were up. She smiled to see the two glasses left on the table. Reaching into the fridge, she brought out the orange juice and poured some into one of the glasses. The clock showed it was just after nine. Not that late really.

"Merry Christmas," she cried, bursting into the lounge. "Hope you've left some champers for me."

Ade looked up from the chair by the fireplace. Rita was sitting on the floor having her shoulders massaged. "I think there may be a wee drop left for you."

Rita smiled at her. "Merry Christmas, sweetheart. You were dead to the world when we looked in on you a little while ago."

"Yeah, well, Gaby's still passed out. So I thought I'd let her sleep on."

"She must have been shattered. I did try not to let her do too much."

89

"I know. Believe me, I know."

The evidence of hastily unwrapped presents lay all around.

"You've opened your stockings." Wil found the champagne bottle by the tree and poured herself a glass. She'd left Gaby's orange juice on the table by the door.

"Sorry, hon. We couldn't wait."

"What are you, five?" She took a sip. "Mm. That's nice." She settled down in the chair opposite to savour more of the bubbly drink. "So, what did Santa bring you?"

Ade looked into the fire and Rita's skin darkened.

"Oh, come on! You guys are too old to be embarrassed."

"And you're too young to know what we might be embarrassed about." Ade shot back.

A knock on the door saved them from any further teasing.

"Come in."

A disheveled looking JJ stood in the doorway. "Sorry to bother you, but I can't find Shelley. I think she's gone out but there's like three feet of snow out there."

"Gone where?" Wil jumped up and went over to the window. "Shit! It's really coming down. I can't see across the lawn. Ade, we'd better get the downstairs fires lit. If it keeps up like this, a power line could go down."

Ade and Rita were both on their feet. "She can't have gone far in this," Ade said. "I'll phone down to the stables."

"She wouldn't have gone there. She doesn't like horses."

Wil wondered, once again, why these two had booked to come here. The image from the day before came to her of Shelley sitting in the lounge hunched over her phone.

"Maybe she just went down the lane to see if she could get a better phone signal."

"She took her coat. But there are no tracks anywhere, either out the front door or the back. And I've looked in all the rooms downstairs."

"Okay. Well, let's go down to your room and see if she's taken anything else with her that might give us a clue." Wil looked over at her friends. "Rita, could you check on Gaby? Ade, can you do the fires?"

They both nodded and Wil headed down the stairs with the distraught JJ in tow.

"I don't understand why she would go out in this," JJ said, opening the door to their room.

Wil looked around. It was very tidy. There was no sign of any Christmas cards or wrapped presents.

"So, did she have a handbag?"

"No. We both had backpacks. Easier for travelling on the train. Wait, hers is gone. It was here by the dresser last night." JJ slumped down into the chair. "Where would she go?"

"I don't know. Look, come down to the study with me. I'll use the phone in there. It doesn't seem too likely, with all this snow, but she might have got a taxi to the station."

Thankfully, Ade had thought to light the fire in the study first. Wil told JJ to sit down and get warm. She went over to the phone and dialled. Once upon a time she had gone to school with David Watson, the only taxi driver within a six mile radius. "Hi, Dave. Merry Christmas to you, too. Bit of a long shot, just wondered, did you pick up a fare from the house earlier today?" She listened, painfully aware that JJ was watching her anxiously. "Oh. Right. Well, that's a good thing. Where did you drop her off?" Another pause while she heard what he had to say. "Uh, huh. Great. You have a good day. Love to Marcie and the kids."

Ade had come in and Wil nodded towards the drinks cabinet. She sat down next to JJ while Ade poured out a large measure of brandy and placed it on the table in front of them.

Wil took a deep breath. "He did pick her up. She booked it yesterday. He hadn't wanted to do it at first, with it being Christmas morning. He's always there for his kids, playing Santa." She looked at the brandy glass, thinking she wouldn't mind a slug herself. "Anyway, Shelley told him she could pay cash and wanted to be picked up at the end of the lane at five."

"Five! But there won't be any trains for hours."

"She didn't go to the train station. He took her to Brighton."

"Brighton! But that's miles away."

"Fifteen miles, and during the day, the drive can take anywhere from thirty minutes to an hour. But at that time of the morning he was able to do the trip quickly, and was back home by six thirty. He says the snow was just starting to come down then. Anyway, he was pleased to have a Christmas bonus and only charged her fifty pounds."

JJ picked up the brandy glass and knocked some back. "Fuck. She must have planned this. I wondered why she wanted to come here. And when we arrived, well you saw what she's been like." She took another drink. "Where did he take her?"

"He dropped her outside The Grand, that's the main hotel on the sea front, and made some comment about hoping she'd enjoy the Christmas lunch there." Wil closed her eyes, not wanting to witness the pain her words were inflicting.

"She said she wasn't staying there but she was meeting someone."

"This is weird," Ade said. She had perched herself on the stone ledge by the fire and was poking at the logs. "Didn't she leave a note or anything?"

JJ shook her head and finished the brandy.

The phone rang. Wil leapt up to get it.

"Oh, hi. Mark. Yeah, we've got everything we need. Good thing we brought the supplies up yesterday." She listened. "Of course. Totally understand. Stay safe."

She put the phone down. "They're not coming for lunch. Figure they need to stay around the pub in case the power goes down."

"Is that likely?" Ade asked.

"It's happened before. We've got a back-up generator but I hope we won't have to use it."

"What about Felicity and Rose?"

"My guess is they will take care of the horses then make their way up here."

"On horseback?"

"No. They have snowshoes." Wil paced over to the window. "It doesn't look like stopping anytime soon." She turned back to look at her distraught guest. "I'm sorry, JJ, but no one will be able to get in or out of here today. I'll bring you some coffee. Have you eaten, yet?"

The woman, hunched into her oversize sweater, just shook her head.

"Um, okay. If you need to make any calls, you're welcome to use this phone. I'll get you some coffee and toast, all right?"

Another nod.

Ade followed Wil out and waited until she'd closed the door behind them.

Wil blew out her cheeks. "What a shit! Who would do that, on Christmas Day?"

"JJ's better off without her, if you ask me."

"Yeah, well, I don't think she's seeing it that way at the moment. Come on, better see about her breakfast."

They arrived in the kitchen to the sound of laughter. Sally and Clare seemed to be sharing a joke, both holding onto the counter and shaking with mirth.

"Merry Christmas! Have you two been at the bubbly already?

Sally turned towards her, tears streaming down her cheeks. "Oh God." She wiped at her cheeks with her sleeve. "You tell them, Clare."

"Oh, they've heard it before, I'm sure." Clare looked over at Wil. "I wanted to go out and play in the snow, but I haven't brought any proper winter gear with me."

"I can sort you out. Rita and I always leave some stuff here," Ade said.

"Well, that's great. You can play all you want later, but I think we should see about clearing some snow out to make the back door accessible." Wil indicated the back door. "Felicity and Rose will come in this way. No point in bothering out the front."

"Okay. You game for that, Clare?"

"Sure."

"Let's get kitted out then."

They headed back down the hallway.

Wil busied herself with the coffee pot.

"Anything I can do to help?" asked Sally, now fully recovered from her laughing fit.

"Um, yeah. Can you do some toast?

"Sure. Breakfast in bed for Gabriella?"

"No. It's for JJ."

"Oh. Is she poorly?"

Wil finished measuring out the grounds. She realised she was going to have to break the news to all the residents. It was going to put a bit of a dampener on the celebrations for the day. Someone had put the turkeys in to cook though; a tantalising aroma was starting to pervade the kitchen. Probably Rita or Teresa. She knew they'd worked out a rota between them to keep Gaby off her feet for at least a good part of the day.

"She's had a bit of a shock. Shelley's gone."

Sally put the bread in the toaster and turned to look at her. "Gone? Where?"

Wil took a deep breath. They'd been in business for fifteen years and this was the first time anyone had done a runner. She told Sally what she knew of the situation.

"Good grief. No wonder she looked so twitchy."

Ade and Clare reappeared both suitably dressed for a polar expedition.

"The shovels are in the cellar. I'll get them. Sally, would you mind taking this to JJ? She's in the study." Without waiting for an answer, Wil set off down the cellar steps. One way or another this was going to be a Christmas to remember.

† 

Enjoying the warmth of her lover's breath on her neck and the comforting feel of her arms around her waist, Candice looked out at the wintry scene from their bedroom window. Whatever had been bothering Mags when they arrived seemed to have magically dissipated. The bluebird had returned. Their evening had ended, or started depending on how you viewed it, with a gentle lovemaking session. Christmas morning had been greeted with a more energetic and passionate encounter.

It was one of the best starts to a Christmas Day she could remember. They had consumed the breakfast she'd brought up to the room and opened their presents. Just a few small things they'd brought with them.

Now they were finally up and dressed, surveying the inviting expanse of snow-covered lawn below. "One small problem, sweetheart."

"What's that?"

"We didn't bring any winter gear with us."

"I'm sure we can borrow something."

When preparing for the trip, they had been assured that the southern part of the UK rarely got much in the way of snow. They weren't likely to need heavy-duty parkas or sheepskin mittens. Now Candice was thinking the waterproof jackets and rain hats they had brought weren't going to provide much in the way of protection from this onslaught of snow. They did have the sweaters and fleece-lined gilets they'd worn for riding the day before, but no proper boots, hats, or gloves.

"Look, *chéri*. Those sculpture things are completely covered. They really do look like horses."

Candice didn't need to turn around to know that her lover was smiling. This was more like the Mags who had first captured her heart, not the one who had returned mentally damaged after her last tour in Afghanistan. She hadn't known much about PTSD before, but she did now as they had both battled with the effects through the last two years. In the darkest times, when it seemed the real Mags was lost, Candice had vowed that she wouldn't give up on her. They would get through this together.

She was thankful for this timely snowfall; it could only bring back happy childhood memories for Mags. Winter holidays spent in the family's chalet when there was always snow at Christmas.

†

JJ was on the phone when Sally arrived in the study. She put the tray on the table and waited for JJ to finish, pleased to be able to have a look at this room, the inner sanctum for Wil and Gabriella, and their intimate circle. Seeing Ade McPherson for the first time had been a shock. Sally hadn't realised she was black. *Wouldn't have expected her to be part of the horsey set—God that was a racist thought!* Sally wandered over to the bookshelves. Of course: a full set of the Amy Ransom books in hardback. She pulled the first one out. Signed, naturally, to Wil. Curiosity getting the better of her, she took out the last one. Number ten had been published posthumously. No signature but the dedication was to Wil and Ade. It would be worth checking the whole series, not just for the dedications but for the acknowledgements that could tell a story as well as providing the names of other people Sally could contact.

Unfortunately, JJ finished her call before Sally could open another book. It would take time anyway. If she looked the titles up on Amazon, she could probably get the info without having to actually buy all the books again. Her last girlfriend had taken Sally's set during their not-very-amicable split, so she couldn't even ask for them back.

She smiled at JJ. "Hi. Wil asked me to bring this in for you. Really sorry to hear about Shelley."

JJ grimaced and sat down. "Yeah, well, I didn't see it coming."

Sally sat down opposite and nodded sympathetically. "That's generally the way. My most recent ex dumped me via Facebook. All my so-called friends knew before I did."

"You would think after five years together, she could have said something. I thought she was just going through a rough time at work."

"Wow. Five years. Two's been my longest so far."

"Can't believe she planned this. Christmas Day for fuck's sake."

Sally wasn't sure what to say to that. She picked up a piece of toast and started munching. JJ didn't seem interested in either the coffee or the food.

"I called my parents. Just wished them a Merry Christmas and told them it was snowing here. They haven't had anything there. I didn't tell them about Shel. They never really liked her anyway."

Wanting to divert a misery fest, Sally looked around the room. "This was Kim Russell's study. She would have written most of her books here."

"What books? Who's Kim Russell?"

"Have you not read her books? That's why most lesbians come here." Sally jumped up and grabbed one of the books she'd been looking at earlier. "Here. Don't get crumbs on it, though. It's a first edition and signed."

JJ looked at the cover. "Oh, yeah. I've seen a couple of the Amy Ransom films. And Clare, she was in some of them, right?"

"Yes. Kim Russell, the writer, lived here. This was her home."

JJ turned the book over and looked at the author photo on the back. "Hm. Not bad looking. Where does she live now?"

"Jesus, I can't believe you don't know anything about her. She's dead. The date's there on the bottom. Died fifteen years ago in a riding accident. So the coroner said, anyway. There was some speculation it was suicide."

"Why would she do that? Looks like she had everything. Rich, successful..."

"Oh, it's well known that she had a drink problem. Apparently she would never admit to being an alcoholic. Rumours are that she was very ill in the months before she died."

Sally was just warming to her topic when the door opened. Wil came in and seemed surprised to see her. Perhaps she had expected her to just dump the tray and leave, like a waitress.

"Have you managed to make your calls, JJ?" she asked.

JJ nodded.

"Well the lounge has warmed up now, if you'd like to go in there." She noticed the book JJ was still holding. "If you want to read any of these, there's another set in the lounge for visitors."

"Of course. Sorry, we were just talking about the books and how exciting it is to be in the place they were written." Sally wondered how it was she always managed to sound like a dipstick when talking to Wil Tyler.

"Oh, she didn't write in here. She had a desk in the master bedroom."

"Which room is that?"

"It was divided into two when we renovated." Wil closed her eyes and Sally thought she wasn't going to say anything else. Then she opened them again and Sally was struck by the depth of green. "The room you're in was where she did her writing. Her desk was in the corner between the windows. She didn't like being distracted by the views."

"Really. That is awesome."

"Yeah. Look, I've got some calls to make. Would you mind...?"

JJ was already on her feet. She picked up the tray and headed for the door. "Thanks for everything. Is it okay if I go into the kitchen? I think I'd like some cereal."

"Yes, of course. Help yourself."

Sally followed JJ out, buoyed by the news that she was sleeping in part of Kim Russell's bedroom.

†

Wil sat down in the spot recently vacated by JJ. The book was lying on the table, Kim's face staring up at her. It was number ten. The photograph filled the back cover, with just the dates underneath: *5 November 1954 − 14 February 1999.*

There was no doubt in her mind that the suicide theory was accurate. The juxtaposition of dates was deliberate, the kind of message Kim knew she would understand. Her mother's birthday, the end. There was also the letter, which only she and Ade had seen. The words she had committed to memory and the last paragraph came into her mind now. She could hear Kim's voice in her head: *"Winterbourne has always been a special place for me. I think it is for you, too. That's why I want you to have it. If you don't want it, then do with it what you wish. But I would like to think you will keep it for me."*

"I'm keeping it for you, Kim," she said aloud, swiping at her eyes.

"Wil!"

Gaby came into the room, moving slowly, with one hand on her protruding belly.

"Babe! Are you okay?" Wil jumped up.

"*Si. Grazie.*"

"*Certo?*"

"*Si.*"

Wil looked into her dark eyes. "Is everything all right?" She put a hand on Gaby's stomach.

"She's moving about some. I'm going to sit down here for a bit. Rita's checking the turkeys."

"You stay here as long as you want. Rita and your mum will have things covered in the kitchen." Wil retrieved the blanket from the alcove and made sure Gaby was comfortably settled with cushions behind her back. She put another log on the fire.

"By the way, Rita says she's going to kill you."

"Oh, why?" Wil returned the book to the shelf and looked back at Gaby.

"Making Ade go out and shovel snow. It'll be your fault if she has a heart attack."

"Ade's as strong as a horse. Anyway, I only wanted them to clear the bit by the kitchen door. I haven't asked them to shovel out the drive."

"Wil?"

"What is it?" Wil knelt down by the sofa and took her hand. It was cold.

"I wanted to thank you properly, you know, for the cradle. And make it up to you for doubting you. But..." she indicated her large lump.

"Last night was wonderful. Just being able to hold you, well, both of you. When madam's made her appearance, we'll have a chance to make up for lost time. Maybe. If you're not too busy breast feeding and things."

"I'll always have time for you, Wil. *Buon Natale, cara!*"

"*Buon Natale.*" Wil kissed her on the lips.

"Hey, you two. Knock it off. There's work to be done."

Wil looked up at Ade, who had barged in, still wearing her outdoor coat with big globs of snow attached to parts of it. "You survived, then."

"Guido's taken over. So Clare and I have been making snow angels. Anyway, Rita wants you to taste the mulled wine. She's not sure about quantity, either."

"Tasting the mulled wine. That's definitely a priority task! All right. I'll be there in a few minutes."

Ade took the hint and left them alone again.

"You haven't opened your presents?"

"Just knowing you love me is all the present I need." Wil brushed a strand of hair away from Gaby's face. "And I have another gift for you. But I reckon it will be this evening before we'll have any time to ourselves again." She kissed the top of Gaby's head. "I'd better go and do Rita's bidding. Can I get you anything?"

"Maybe some water, when you have a minute."

"Okay. You keep your feet up. We'll all be fine."

Gaby's eyes were closing, and before Wil reached the door, she could tell Gaby was asleep.

†

Trapped in a house full of women. Guido wasn't sure how he'd let himself be talked into it. He tackled the path by the side of the house. The last time he'd seen snow like this was when they had a family holiday at Lake Como, too many years ago to count. Hard as those times had been, working year round on the farm, providing for his wife and kids, he missed them, missed the constant activity and laughter. Their youngest son had taken over the day-to-day running of the farm and encouraged his parents to take extended holidays. Didn't want his old man hovering about, telling him how he should do things.

And now that Gaby was having a baby, he was sure Teresa would want to spend more time here. He found the continual dampness chilling though. Shoveling his way through the heavy white stuff was the first time he'd been properly warm since they arrived. His wife coped better, but she had more fat on her. Not that he would ever tell her that.

A sturdy splat on his back made him look up. Felicity Evans was standing a few feet away, another ball of snow shaping in her hands, a big grin on her face. "Gotcha, old man!"

He threw the shovel to one side and picked up a handful ready for attack. "*Puttana*! You pay!"

Another ball hit his chest. He looked around to see Rose giving him an innocent smile.

"Not fair." He held up his hands.

Felicity stomped the snow off her snowshoes onto his neatly cleared path. She bent down to unstrap the shoes from her boots, but squealed when the cold snow Guido placed on her neck started to trickle down her back. She straightened up.

"That was uncalled for."

"I said you pay."

"We paid you enough the other night."

Rose had removed her shoes and leant them against the wall. "Enough squabbling, children. You know, a better way to clear some of this snow would be to make a snowman."

"Oh, no. We'll make a snow horse. With Guido's help we can make a really big one."

Guido looked from one to the other to see if they were pulling his leg. "A snow horse. *Un cavallo?*"

Felicity didn't look like she was joking this time. "Yes. Look, if we start rolling here, in zigzags, we'll have this snow cleared in no time. Show him, Rose"

†

The mulled wine tasted as good as Wil knew Gaby would have made it. And Rita had produced enough to last two days. Wil looked out the back door to see if Guido would like a taster to warm up and was taken aback by the sight of the three figures struggling with a large ball of snow at least four feet high. They were trying to push it next to another one.

"Looks like they need help."

Wil turned to find Marguerite standing behind her. She was bundled up in what looked like her own sheepskin jacket, complete with gloves and scarf.

"Hope you don't mind. We didn't bring anything for snow."

"No, that's okay. And, yes, I think you'd better go and help them. The silly old fools."

Mags ran out to add her weight to the effort. They managed to push the unwieldy ball into place and then broke off in different directions to shouted instructions from Felicity. Guido and Mags started rolling out what looked like elongated snow shapes. Rose marched across to the kitchen and called out to Wil.

"Have we got any spare lids?"

"Lids?"

"Yes. Off a jar, preferably black."

"You could have the ones off the jam and marmalade jars. I can cover them over with cling film. Wait there." Wil retrieved the lids from the breakfast items still on the table and handed them over.

"Oh, and we'll need to borrow the stepladder as well."

Wil fetched the short stepladder from behind the pantry door. "What are you making?"

"It's a snow horse."

Wil closed the door and leant against it with her eyes closed, forcing herself to take deep breaths. Was everyone conspiring today to remind her of Kim? She remembered that year when it snowed and Kim had told her that her editor, an ardent feminist, would never forgive her if she made a snow*man*. They created two horses facing each other, and played at jousting. Wil had never laughed so much. It had been magical. Probably the last time she and Kim and Grace were truly happy together.

   …Wanting desperately to create a family Christmas atmosphere, Wil had pestered Kim into decorating the entrance hall and dragging in the biggest spruce tree they could find in the woods, with some added horsepower, to finish off the Christmas decor in style. She was nineteen but she wanted the whole experience, creating a childhood festivity she'd never had. Kim read one of the Narnia books to her; amazed to find that Wil had never read them as a child. Wil felt it was an appropriate metaphor of her life until then—a place where it was always winter, but never Christmas—until the spell was broken. That year the magic of Narnia surrounded them.

   By the next Christmas, the magic had gone. Grace was very much in demand and immersed in her television work. Kim went to Australia for the filming of the fourth Amy Ransom book, staying for two months and having an affair with one of the actresses. Wil never really understood Kim's relationship with Grace. She remembered talking with Ade about it in the early days, about how obsessed they were with each other. But apart from when they were making love, they drove each other crazy. Wil had to acknowledge that Grace had tried, really tried, to tolerate Kim's drinking. Kim wouldn't admit to being an alcoholic; she said it was her creative juice.

   Through all the upheavals with Kim and Grace, Ade had been her rock. When the going got tough, Wil would turn up at Ade's and always found a welcome. Ade moderated her drinking when Rita was around and, unlike

Kim, was able to adapt to a change in her lifestyle. And from the mid 1990s, Ade was much in demand, working for large corporate businesses, preparing their computer systems to cope with the "Millennium Bug." So she had less time to "play" with Kim and indulge in wild binges.

Wil had asked Ade how the two of them met. They seemed like such an unlikely pairing. And when Ade told her the story, it seemed a strange place for either of them to be— Greenham Common in 1983.

"What were you doing there?"

"I was there because I believed, still do, in living in a nuclear-free world. Kim was writing an article for a right-wing newspaper. Opposite ends of the spectrum. I ended up rescuing her from an angry mob of peaceniks." Ade had closed her eyes, remembering the scene. "It was a calm evening in May, really lovely, clear blue sky, but cold. A group of us were sitting around a campfire just gassing, you know. Then this scruffy looking white woman appeared, okay most of us looked pretty rough after weeks of camping out, but Kim looked particularly unkempt, like she'd been dragged through a bush backwards. At first she just sat and listened to the talk, then someone said something about 'that bitch in Number Ten' and Kim lit up. She told everyone in no uncertain terms that Mrs Thatcher was a great woman and deserved to be recognised as such instead of being reviled by her own kind. Next thing you know, she's toe-to-toe with one of the biggest dykes in the group. I have to say I didn't think Kim would stand up to her, but she didn't back down and gave as good as she got. It would have been a fair fight but others joined in and started kicking and punching her when she went down. I couldn't sit and watch that, so I waded in and got her out of there."

"I can't see Kim as a fighter."

"She was always tougher than she looked. She used to beat me at arm wrestling."

"No way!"

"Yeah. It got us thrown out of one bar. People had taken bets—and the top money was on me. When Kim won, the losers accused us of setting them up. It didn't matter what we said, they just thought we'd fixed it. Going out with Kim was never dull."…

Wil started when a hand landed on her shoulder. She opened her eyes to find Rita looking at her, concerned.

"Are you all right, Wil?"

"Yes. Just, I don't know. Sometimes I wonder, what might have been…"

Rita knew what she meant without being told. "You couldn't have done anything to help if you had been here. And my guess is she didn't want you here. Come on, Wil. Snap out of it. We've got work to do."

"Yeah. I'm just going to go and check on Gaby."

"Okay. Oh, and Wil," Rita stopped her and pulled her into a hug, "that cradle is wonderful. Well done."

"Do I get a gold star, teach?"

Rita let go of her. "You'll get a smack round the head if you're not back here in five minutes to help with the veg."

Wil danced out of her way. "You're not allowed to hit me, miss."

Rita flicked a tea towel at her. "Get gone. And find out where Ade's hiding out while you're at it."

†

The lounge was quiet with only the flames crackling through the logs in the grate. With no Internet access, Sally decided it was a good time to do as Wil had suggested and take a look at Kim Russell's books. The first book, she already knew, was dedicated to her uncle, Philip Russell, the original owner of Winterbourne House. Opening the second one on the shelf, she quickly flicked through the opening pages. First edition, published in 1988. Dedicated to Thelma Barton. Well, well. Maybe the old woman had more to tell about her own relationship with the writer. Or did it say more about Kim, that she didn't dedicate it to any members of her family, a close friend, or lover?

Checking through the drawers of the desk in the corner of the room, Sally found a sheaf of lined A4 notepaper and an assortment of pens. She piled the books on the table in publication order and started a list. It hadn't occurred to her before, but the dedications could provide a useful timeline, a guide to the important relationships in Kim's life.

When she'd finished, the list looked like this:

| Book | Publication date | Dedication |
|------|------------------|------------|
| AR1: | 1987 | Philip |
| AR2: | 1988 | Thelma |
| AR3: | 1989 | Ginny |
| AR4: | 1990 | Ade |
| AR5: | 1991 | Grace |
| AR6: | 1995 | Glen |
| AR7: | 1996 | Clare |
| AR8: | 1997 | Blake |
| AR9: | 1998 | Antony |
| AR10: | 1999 | Wil and Ade |

Sally replaced the books carefully on the shelf, making sure they were back in the right order. She kept out number 7 and sat down in the seat nearest the fire with her notes.

She was familiar with all except for two of the male names. Who were Glen and Antony? That was something to be explored. Of the women, Ade was her closest friend; Sally knew that. But numbers three, five, and seven were all lovers—Ginny, Grace, Clare. Number eight, Blake, she wasn't sure about. There had been a suggestion that the actress was bisexual and had publicly kissed Kim at her fortieth birthday party—a photograph that made it into all the papers, not just the sensation-seeking tabloids. From the reports Sally had ferreted out from the archives, this had led to the first break-up with television presenter, Grace Green. Shortly after that, Kim had gone to Australia where book number four was being filmed, and met Clare.

Then there were the missing years, the hiatus between 1991 and 1995. Kim hadn't stopped writing. Sally knew there was another series the writer had started. A different heroine, Cary Fontaine. When she'd looked the books up on Amazon, she had found that they were out of print with no eBook versions available. Sally went over to the bookcase and looked through the shelves again. If Wil possessed the books they weren't on public display. She would have to gain access to the study again.

It was all very complicated but Sally was sure it would make a good story, if she could just get these people to talk. Clare had deflected her questions the night before, but there had been a definite softening in her attitude towards Sally. Maybe a bit more Christmas spirit would help get things moving. That, and the fact they were all trapped here. The snow had started to fall again.

†

The romp in the snow had been great fun. Clare's only experiences with the white stuff had been on the occasional family ski trips to Jindabyne in the Snowy Mountains. Winter holidays in June, not December.

She left Ade at the back door and removed her wet outdoor gear before heading into the kitchen. Helping herself to another coffee was on her mind, but the preparations for the Christmas lunch were well underway and it wasn't possible to get near the coffee pot. Rita, however, welcomed her with a big smile and offered a mug of mulled wine. It seemed Ade's partner was starting to thaw towards her. Or maybe it was just an overflow of Christmas spirit from tasting too much festive drink.

Clare accepted the mug gratefully and smiled back.

"There's a fire in the lounge," Rita said. "We'll be having the pre-lunch get together there in about half an hour."

"Great. Thanks, I'll go and warm up my toes."

"Where's Ade?"

"She said she was going to see if she could find the cross-country skis in the cellar."

"Right. Anything to avoid actual work." Rita turned back to the vegetables awaiting her attention on the counter.

The words weren't said with any rancour. Clare figured Ade was big enough to fight her own battles anyway, and headed down the passageway to find sanctuary in the lounge. Sally was already there, writing on a pad, which she hastily covered over when she saw her. But not before Clare had seen what looked like a list with dates and names.

She sat down opposite and stretched her legs towards the open fire. "What are you writing?"

"Oh, nothing important."

Clare took a sip of her mulled wine before putting the mug on the side table. "Don't take up acting, Sally. Because you're pretty bad at telling porkies."

"Okay. It's just a bit of research."

"For what?"

"I'm writing a book, if you must know."

"Right." Clare glanced at the book in front of the other woman. "About Kim Russell if I'm not mistaken."

"What makes you think that?"

Clare smiled. "You've been fishing for information ever since you got here."

"Am I that transparent?"

"Yes. 'Fraid so."

"Well, it's going to be a short book, seeing as no one here will talk to me, yourself included. Everyone clams up when KR is mentioned."

The mulled wine was really very good. Clare didn't normally like this traditional Christmas beverage, but Rita's concoction was more like a warm sangria than any she'd had before. Hopefully she was planning to bring it through for the other guests to sample at the pre-lunch gathering. Licking her lips after finishing the drink, Clare looked over at Sally who was contemplating her notes sadly.

"So, what's on the list?"

"I was looking through the AR books to see who they were dedicated to. Seems to offer some clues about relationships." Sally indicated the book on the table. "This one, for example, is dedicated to you, published in 1996, which is after you met Kim. On the set of the filming for book number four, wasn't it?"

Clare closed her eyes. Making love with Kim for the first time. It was a scene she often replayed in her mind.

...Kim had invited her up to her room even though she could barely stand at that point. Clare wasn't much better, having drunk her fair share of champagne on the boat. After some initial fumbling, they had managed to get their clothes off themselves and each other and engage in something that might have passed for sex if either of them could remember what they were doing. The alcohol may have dulled the activity on that occasion but the desire hadn't been diminished. The next day, in her dressing room on the set, Clare had shamelessly seduced the writer, removing her costume in front of her provocatively. Kim had succumbed willingly to her advances, sucking eagerly on one breast while seeking to help her out of her tight leather trousers with her hands. Even thinking of that scene now could arouse her...

Clare opened her eyes again to find Sally staring at her.

"I thought you'd nodded off."

"I think the wine's taking effect."

"See, you're doing it again."

"What?"

"Avoiding talking about her."

"It's my story and it's not for sale."

"Okay. Maybe you can help me out with this, then." Sally picked up her list. "There are two male names I can't figure out here. AR6 is dedicated to Glen and AR9 to Antony."

"Well, that's easy enough. She had a horse called Glenmorangie, although most people who knew her thought she'd dedicated the book to the whisky of the same name. And Antony is Grace Green's father. He's in *Who's Who* if you want to look him up. Kim had a close relationship with him, helping him come out of the closet in his later years."

"Wow. That's something I didn't know. So Grace's father was gay. That wasn't mentioned in her autobiography."

"No. I don't imagine it was." Clare was saved from revealing anything more by the entrance of Candice and Marguerite followed closely by Ade carrying the urn full of mulled wine.

†

JJ returned to her room and stared out of the window. Four heavily clad figures were grouped around two large mounds of snow. It took her a moment to register what she was seeing. They weren't making a snowman. It looked like they were trying to assemble a horse. The long neck and head was giving them trouble, getting it to stay in place.

She shook her head and turned back to survey the room. How had she not heard Shelley leave? She hadn't drunk that much the night before. Maybe Shel had drugged her.

Her gaze stopped on the armchair. Where was the suitcase? When they'd arrived she remembered Shelley putting it behind the chair after unpacking. But what had she unpacked? She only recalled her putting underwear in a drawer. JJ had taken her stuff out first, leaving Shelley to arrange her own. She had teased her about the amount of clothing she'd brought but hadn't thought anything of it. Shelley always packed more than she needed and would then complain she had nothing to wear. JJ's wardrobe mainly consisted of jeans and t-shirts for work. For this trip she had just brought a pair of smarter jeans and two brightly coloured shirts to wear for the festive meals.

She checked behind the chair and gasped. The small pile of wrapped gifts lay there, the presents she'd brought for Shelley so she would have something to open on Christmas morning. On top was a letter-sized envelope with JJ in large letters written in green ink—Shel's choice of pen was always green.

Picking up the envelope she experienced a wave of nausea. Sitting down in the chair she closed her eyes and waited for the feeling to pass. A few deep breaths and she opened her eyes to study the envelope. It looked too innocuous to hold the words that she knew could only cause her more pain. Unable to face the inevitable, she went over to the bed and lay down, letting her tears soak into the pillow that still smelt of her departed lover.

†

Guido looked resplendent in his Santa costume. Years earlier, Wil had tried to persuade him that lesbians would prefer a female Santa, but he'd told her not to mess with traditions, and anyway Gaby had made the outfit so he was wearing it.

The residents were all rounded up and gathered in the lounge, some of them already on their second or third mugs

115

of mulled wine. Wil stopped Guido before he entered the room.

"Just need to check your sack, Santa."

He raised his bushy eyebrows, only his eyes showing above the long white beard.

Wil removed one of the wrapped presents. "We're one short," she explained. "After you've done your bit, I'm going to make an announcement."

She entered the room ahead of him and nodded to Ade who started the music playing, a string quartet version of "Deck the Halls." Wil stepped aside as Guido marched in, sack over his shoulder, uttering a convincing "Ho, Ho, Ho" in his deep, throaty voice. Felicity told her he practiced loudly while helping with the mucking out of a morning, and she'd asked him to stop because it was frightening the horses.

Santa made his rounds, handing out presents, eyes twinkling. Wil had to admit Guido made a fine job of it. He looked over at her questioningly, shaking his sack. One present left.

"Oh, I guess JJ hasn't made it down. Leave it with me, Santa. I'll make sure she gets it."

Gaby caught her eye and smiled. That was all Wil needed to help her get through the next few minutes. When Guido made his final bow and left the room, Ade turned the music off.

Wil glanced around at the assembled family and guests, all present except Felicity. "Would anyone like more mulled wine?" There was a general shake of heads, so she continued. "I have a few announcements. It's probably good that JJ's not here right now. She may or may not be joining us for lunch. Shelley left this morning, very early. She managed to get a taxi to take her to Brighton before the snow came down."

Into the shocked silence, Wil heard someone mutter, "She was a miserable cow anyway. Good riddance."

Taking a deep breath, Wil continued. "We will, of course, carry on with our Christmas programme. Lunch will be served in half an hour." She looked over at Rita for confirmation. "We do have enough food and drink to see us through the next few days. Communication with the outside world is non-existent as the phone line has now gone down, and the Wi-Fi signal has died completely. We have a back-up generator, should the power go off, and plenty of wood for the fireplaces."

"I guess the Christmas walk through the woods is off."

This was from Sally. Wil was sure she had been the one who made the comment about Shelley.

"Yes. However, Ade found two sets of cross-country skis in the cellar should anyone wish to take some exercise. I was planning to root them out anyway, in case Gaby decides to give birth anytime in the next twenty-four hours. Although Felicity assures me she's birthed enough foals to know what to do."

"How appropriate! But we'll have to get Gaby down to the stables to make it authentic." Ade had a mischievous gleam in her eye.

"You do no such thing!" Teresa wrapped a protective arm around her daughter. "This baby will not be born in stable."

"Joke, T." Ade held up her hands.

Rita stood. "I'm going to check on the veg." She pointed at Gaby who was making a move to stand. "You stay there. Rose and I can manage."

When she'd gone, Wil looked around at the assembly. "Okay, I guess that's all for now. Not long until lunch is ready. Ade, would you mind checking on JJ?"

Ade nodded and Wil sat down on the hearth and stared into the fireplace. This was going to be a strange Christmas Day. The snow would distract most of the guests but she wasn't sure how lunch would go if JJ chose to join them.

†

A knock on the door brought JJ round and she sat up quickly, realising she'd fallen asleep. The door opened and the tall black woman, whom she thought was called Ade, came in carrying a mug.

"Sorry to barge in. Wil asked me to check on you."

"Um, yeah. I must've fallen asleep."

Ade held out the mug. "Brought you some mulled wine. It's rather good."

JJ accepted the mug. It certainly smelled enticing. "Thanks."

"Look, we know you might not feel like joining us for lunch. Rita will put something aside for you if you don't want to come down."

Sipping at the warm liquid, JJ considered the offer. "I don't know. I suppose everyone knows about Shelley."

"Yes." Ade sat down on the edge of the bed. "Wil told the group just now."

"She left me a letter." JJ nodded towards the armchair.

"Oh."

"I haven't opened it. Could you?"

"You want me to read it?"

JJ nodded, not trusting herself to speak.

"Okay." Ade covered the distance to the chair with a single stride. She picked up the envelope and sat down in the chair to open it.

JJ drank more of the mulled wine, watching over the rim of the mug as Ade scanned the contents of the single folded sheet of paper. After what seemed like forever she looked across at JJ and sighed.

"Not a great letter writer, your Shel. It seems she met someone at a conference and they've decided they want to live together. I'm sorry."

"A conference? Oh yeah. She went to a big real estate event in Birmingham in September. Fuck! You must think I'm a total idiot. I didn't have a clue."

"Shit happens. Usually when we least expect it."

"Yeah, but Christmas Day!"

"I know. Look, it's okay if you want to stay up here."

"No!" JJ stood abruptly. "I'm not going to let her ruin everything. Give me a few minutes. I'll just freshen up."

"That's the spirit. See you downstairs." Ade took the empty mug from her and left.

Splashing water on her face, JJ studied her face in the mirror. She could do this.

## Chapter Four

### Christmas Lunch

Sally wondered when she was going to have another chance to get Clare on her own. *Damned inconvenient all this Christmas stuff.* She had been on the verge of gaining some important info when everyone arrived for the pre-lunch meeting.

The bombshell about Shelley's defection set Candice off and even her previously verbally challenged partner was joining in. They were now engaged in animated chat with Gabriella and her mother. Marguerite was expressing herself with much arm waving as well.

Sally ripped the paper off the present and found herself looking at a framed colour print of the front of Winterbourne House in summer, everything in full bloom, a startling contrast to how the place looked now with all the snow. Sally glanced over at Clare. She was also looking at the photo in her hands. Her face had the faraway look she'd had in the moments before the meeting when Sally had asked her about how she first met Kim Russell.

It wasn't likely she would get anything more out of Clare right now. Maybe if she offered to help in the kitchen she could pick up some tidbits. Ade McPherson was someone she desperately wanted to talk to, but it seemed she was going to have to get past the formidable Rita first.

Just when she'd decided to put this plan into action, the door opened and JJ arrived. The sudden silence as she entered the room was embarrassing, to say the least.

Clare, who moments before looked like she was in another world, was the first to react.

"Hi JJ. Would you like some mulled wine?"

"No, thanks. Ade brought me some. It was very good, but I guess there will be more wine with the meal."

Sally thought she sounded better than she looked. Probably still in shock. She scooted over on the sofa to make room for her.

"What's that?" JJ pointed to the picture still in her hands.

"Oh, it's a Christmas present. We all got one. I guess there's one for you as well."

JJ snorted. "Great. But I don't think I'll be wanting a memento of this place."

Candice, as usual, didn't hold back. "We're all really sorry to hear about Shelley."

There was another uncomfortable silence before JJ spoke again. "Well, I didn't see it coming. What I don't know is how she managed to take the suitcase with her without making enough noise to wake me up this morning."

Clare coughed. "Was it a blue case with red trim?"

"Yes."

"I saw it in the hall cupboard last night when I got my coat to go outside to look at the stars."

Silence again.

This was going to be a fun Christmas meal, Sally decided. Maybe they should play "Truth or Dare" and they could all tell stories of past relationships gone wrong.

JJ seemed to have read her mind as her next words indicated. "Look, I don't want to spoil anything for all of you. Please, just act normally. I might be a bit quiet, but honestly I would rather be here with everyone than sitting on my own in my room."

"Good for you!" Candice might have been planning to say more, but Mags who was looking much perkier today, gripped her partner's leg and Candice turned to give her a "what-the-fuck" look. At least that's what it looked like to Sally.

†

Wil poked at the fire and decided another log was needed. JJ's entrance had caused an initial stir but glancing around at the group after replacing the fireguard, she thought everyone looked like they had already eaten a large meal. The only sound was from Teresa, who still had her arm around Gaby, and was talking to her softly in Italian. Ade, standing by the music console, caught her eye and grimaced. The usual party games they had planned on playing after the guests had consumed lunch, watched the Queen's speech, and awakened from various comatose states, weren't going to fly with this crowd.

Felicity appeared in the doorway and indicated with the briefest of head movements that she wanted her. Wil met her in the hall.

"What's up?"

"Fetched the dogs. They're in the study. The Lodge is too cold for them to stay there."

"That's okay. Good idea. You and Rose should stay here tonight as well."

"Ahead of you there. Already settled in."

Wil smiled at the older woman. Even with the work put into the guest house venture over the years by herself, Gaby, Ade and Rita, she knew none of it would have been successful without Felicity's quiet support and wise counsel.

"I'm going to check on the wine. The red should probably be uncorked now."

"Guido's on it." Felicity paused and Wil waited, knowing from long experience there was more to come. "Thirteen."

"Thirteen what?"

"There will be thirteen for lunch," she said, in the patient tone of voice she usually reserved for training young horses.

"Yes, I know. I did the table setting."

"So, I will not be joining you. I'll eat with the dogs."

"Felicity! It's just a number. You can't sit on your own on Christmas Day."

"I can. Raffi and Daisy are good company."

Wil shook her head, knowing there was no use trying to talk her out of it. "Fine. I'll remove your place at the table. Will you be sharing a cracker with your dining companions?"

"No. They don't like the noise. And they won't wear the hats."

"Probably tell better jokes. Believe me, I would love to join you. It's going to be hard work generating a party atmosphere now."

"Women! Nothing but trouble."

Watching the old woman stomp down the passage to the kitchen, Wil shook her head and turned the other way to go into the dining room. She reset the table so the settings were evenly spaced and checked the place-name cards again. Not everyone would be happy with the seating arrangement but it was the best she could do with the reduced numbers. If Mark and Toby had been able to make it, and Shelley hadn't done a bunk, they would have had two tables. With the more intimate number, now twelve, one table seemed a better option. She had put JJ between Clare and Ade. They would treat her gently. Sally might not be too thrilled with having Marguerite and Rose on either side of her, only being able to gaze across the table at Clare. Rita, Teresa, and Guido were seated at the end of the table nearest the door for access to the kitchen. She and Gaby were seated at the other end. Wil felt she was taking a hit for the team by placing Candice at her side and Mags at Gaby's. With any luck, though, she might not be required to contribute much to the conversation.

The two space heaters were helping to warm up the room. By the time everyone had more food and drink in them, they weren't likely to feel the cold. As long as there wasn't a power failure, keeping the house heated wasn't too much of a problem. And they could issue more blankets for the guest rooms.

She glanced out the window. The snow was falling softly again. If it kept up like this, it would take a week to clear the driveway.

†

When everyone was seated, Ade glanced around the table and counted heads. Rose and Teresa were in the kitchen, and Rita and Wil were just bringing in the starters. Guido was pouring wine. But there were only twelve places set so that was the number expected. Had Felicity done a runner as well? Or was she down at the stables?

Ade tried to catch Wil's eye but she was listening to something Sally was saying. Probably complaining about the seating plan. She would just have to put up with being placed between Mags and Rose, only being able to shout across the table if she wanted to talk to Clare. The woman was well named, Hunter. She was keeping tabs on Clare, that was certain. Ade turned her attention to JJ. She looked better than she had in the bedroom earlier. But she must still be in shock.

"So, what does JJ stand for?"

"Jane Jones. Not very original, is it? I only answered to JJ from the time I started Kindergarten."

"No middle name?"

"Sure. Jacintha, would you believe? I could be JJJ, but that was a J too far."

Ade laughed. "I can sympathise. My given name is Adriana. Too many syllables for my liking. I couldn't even say it until I was six and by then Ade had stuck."

Candice had been listening and piped up, "Names are important. I don't like mine being shortened to Candy." She turned to Gaby. "Have you chosen a name for your baby?"

"Heather is the favourite at the moment."

"Hm. An earthy name for a Capricorn. And will she have a middle name?"

"Teresa, after my mother."

"And will she have your surname or have you combined them?"

Did Candice really not have a social filter? Ade was prepared to jump in but Gaby wasn't easily intimidated.

"Combined?"

"Yes, you know. A lot of couples put their names together when they get married. Hyphenated. Like me and Mags would be Hennessy-Bouchard."

Ade was prepared to kick Candice under the table, push her off the chair if necessary.

"We're not married." Gaby looked down at her plate and pushed the parsley garnish to one side.

"Oh, I guess I thought…"

Luckily what she thought was interrupted by Wil and the others returning from the kitchen to take their seats. The low-level hum of conversation increased in volume as crackers were pulled and glasses raised for toasts. Ade unfolded the green hat she had fished out of the split cardboard of her half of the cracker and placed it on her head. She glanced across at Rita but she was engrossed in a tug of war with Rose. The cracker they were attempting to pull finally came apart with only a dismal pop. Rose pounced on the trinket that fell out with an agility that belied her age. It was a set of tiny screwdrivers and Rita pretended to be disappointed.

Ade shook out the contents of her broken cracker and a miniature tape measure fell out. "Where did you get the crackers from, Wil? A hardware store? They're full of do-it-yourself kit for little people."

"Is that a size-ist comment, Ms McPherson?"

"Not at all, shorty."

Mags piped up. "These are great." She was inspecting the tiny scissors in her hand. "My family didn't do crackers."

"That's terrible. It's not Christmas without a cracker." JJ's words reverberated around the table. Ade looked at her. She seemed to be holding herself together well. Unlike everyone else who appeared to be holding their collective breaths.

"No, it's not," Ade said, to break the sudden silence. Recalling JJ's enthusiasms for the truly awful cracker jokes, Ade picked up her slip of paper and read out the question. "Who inspects Santa's workshop?"

JJ's face lit up with her first smile of the day. "Oh, that's an easy one. The Elf and Safety Officer." She scrabbled around in the discarded cracker pieces to find her joke. "Okay. Who gives presents to good little sharks?"

A general murmuring and shaking of heads was quickly followed by JJ's triumphant, "Santa Jaws!"

"Of course." Ade glanced around the table and caught Rita's eye. "Do you remember when you were stopped by airport security trying to take Christmas crackers into Amsterdam?"

Rita gave her a stern look. "I don't think everyone needs to hear that story."

"Oh yes we do!" Wil called out.

"Okay." Ignoring Rita's head shake, Ade continued. "Well, we were visiting one of Rita's old university friends and as a treat she thought of taking a box of Christmas crackers. They were posh ones, from Harrods, weren't they, dear?"

Rita glared at her, arms folded across her chest.

Undeterred, Ade carried on. "It was a lovely box of six crackers and Rita was carrying them in her hand luggage so they wouldn't be crushed. So, her bag goes through the scanner and there's a bit of a delay while another official is called over and they look at the screen. Then they look at Rita. She explains that the crackers all have a present inside. However, the problem is that one of them has a bottle opener in it. And they can't allow this to go through. I don't know what they thought she was going to do with it. Anyway, possibly because she was smartly dressed and stayed calm while she asked them to please not confiscate all the crackers, they eventually relented. But it meant they had to put the box through the scanner three times to identify which one had the bottle opener. And she was allowed to take the other five. This took some time and the people queued up behind her were not amused."

"I'll bet." Clare looked over at Rita. "Weren't they concerned about the stuff on the cardboard strips that makes the bang when the crackers are pulled apart? I mean that's a chemical and is probably highly unstable. More of a security risk than a tiny bottle opener, I would have thought."

Rita smiled. "Yes, I thought that. I was surprised they let me take them in the end. But I wasn't going to argue."

"So, we're dining with a cracker smuggler," Candice said, and everyone laughed, including Rita.

In between bites of the smoked salmon starter, there were further readings of inane questions and equally inane answers. Ade noticed that Teresa didn't join in but Guido was happy to read out her joke as well as his own. The older Brunettis were, she knew, more religiously inclined than their daughter. If Teresa wasn't so concerned that Gaby was going to give birth at anytime, she would have gone to the midnight mass held at the village's Catholic church the previous evening.

Ade sincerely hoped that little Heather would delay her arrival into the world. The Harris's farm was a good ten-minute drive away, but no vehicles would be going anywhere with the amount of snow now on the ground. Wil was worried enough without the thought of having to rely on Felicity's foaling skills and Teresa's own birthing experiences.

†

Clare was enjoying the food and the company. Wil had, she thought, excelled herself with the seating arrangements, having managed to separate her from both Candice and Sally. Guido was to her right, at the head of the table, with JJ seated on her left.

Once the preliminaries were over with the crackers, she realised there was someone missing. As if reading her thoughts, Guido suddenly looked up and directed the question at Rose. "Where's the other old woman?"

"She's with the dogs. They're in the study."

"Why not bring them in here?" Clare asked.

Rose leant over the table and whispered, "She didn't want to sit at a table of thirteen."

"*Sensato!*" Teresa interjected forcefully.

"Superstitious nonsense, if you ask me," Rose said, in a louder voice.

"*Malagurato.*" Seeing Clare's look of incomprehension, Teresa carried on in her unique mix of English and Italian. "It was unlucky for our Lord, Jesus. *L'ultima Cena.* No?"

"I guess so." Clare didn't want to get drawn into a debate on religion. Her parents had taken her to their

Anglican church but when they wanted to send her to confirmation classes she rebelled. By that time she was well into her martial arts training and was immersing herself in the sayings of Khalil Gibran and the Tao.

Guido deflected the impending conversation with a sudden burst of laughter. He looked at her and said, "Gone to the dogs. That is right phrase?"

Clare smiled at him. "Yes."

"Ha. Old woman gone to the dogs. *Perfetto!*" He attacked his smoked salmon enthusiastically.

"I like your snow horse," Clare said, in an attempt to steer the conversation to a more neutral topic.

"*Magnifico, si!*"

JJ decided to join in. "I saw you making that. It looks fantastic."

"Well, it was a good way to clear the snow," Rose said.

"And to give people heart attacks," Rita added, glancing meaningfully across the table at Ade. But Ade was talking to Candice and didn't notice.

"If we want to get the cars out, we'll have to do the same all the way down the drive." Rose ignored Rita's remark.

"That would be amazing." JJ waved her arms enthusiastically. "You could have a parade of horses all the way along."

"She was joking." Rita gave her a stern look.

Clare finished her salmon and sat back in her chair. "Well, it would be one way to work off lunch."

"It's not going to happen," Rita said, firmly. "Tom Harris, a neighbouring farmer, will come along with his tractor to clear the drive. As soon as he can clear his own, of course."

"I hope he come soon," Teresa interjected. "*La bambina*, not long now."

Rita put a reassuring hand on her arm. "He will. Don't worry." She stood. "Time to bring on the turkey."

"Can I help?" Clare asked.

"No. You're a guest. We've got it covered."

And they did. Clare watched as they moved as a team. Teresa stayed where she was, but Guido got up to help Rose and Wil clear plates. She guessed he was taking on the traditional male role of carving the turkey. Her guess proved correct when he came back from the kitchen bearing a large platter with a very large cooked bird on it. He wielded the carving knife expertly and asked who wanted breast. She didn't dare look at anyone else when he said this but she thought she heard a few stifled giggles.

†

The turkey meat was tender and there was plenty of gravy. Candice wasn't a big fan of turkey, grateful that the Canadian Thanksgiving holiday was in October not the end of November like the American one. Only a month between turkey feasts wasn't a lot to be thankful for in her opinion. And the Brits didn't have a Thanksgiving holiday. As for Brussels sprouts, they could have been left off the menu completely as far as she was concerned. Stewed kale didn't take as long to prepare and would have been as popular.

She checked on Mags, pleased to see she was enjoying an animated conversation with Gabriella. If the woman weren't nine months pregnant and clearly in love with her partner, Candice would be worried. From her position, she could see that Wil and Gaby were holding hands under the table.

Wil seemed to be watching everything, eyes darting around the table, no doubt hoping she hadn't forgotten anything. She turned her serious green-eyed gaze on Candice. "Did you enjoy the ride, yesterday?"

"Yes, we both did. It's lovely countryside around here."

"Well, it looks like we won't be able to take the horses out for a bit with all the snow."

"No. I guess not. Running this place must keep you busy. Do you ever have any holidays, time to yourselves?"

"We usually go back to Italy a few times a year, spend time with Gaby's family. During quiet periods we'll spend two or three nights in London, going to shows, catching up with friends."

"So, when do you plan to get married?" Candice stifled a yell as a well-aimed kick landed painfully on her ankle. She turned to Ade who dramatically drew her hand across her throat. "What, I…" She looked back at Wil who was taking a sip of wine and staring into space.

"I was thinking of making a start on clearing the drive after lunch," Ade said.

"Best not let Rita hear you say that," countered Wil. "Anyway, we might as well wait until it stops snowing."

Candice recovered her composure. The topic of marriage was off limits it seemed. "If we all pitch in, it needn't be too much of a strain on anyone."

Mags called across the table. "It's the worst thing you can do after a big meal. Just asking for a heart attack."

"The voice of experience. Better listen to her. We don't get much snow in Vancouver but Montreal's another matter."

"We weren't planning any strenuous activities after lunch," Wil said. "Watching the Queen's speech is an option and we do have a selection of DVDs."

"Isn't there a soccer match on?" asked Mags.

"Not today. There will be tomorrow, as long as the pitches aren't under three feet of snow."

Candice looked down at her plate, surprised to see that she'd not only eaten all the turkey but several sprouts as well.

Rita called out to ask if anyone wanted more of anything. With the general shaking of heads and murmurs of "no thanks, couldn't eat another thing," she and Rose got up to start clearing the table.

Wil pushed back her chair and collected the plates either side of her.

"Can I help?" Candice asked.

"No, we're good. Ade, can you bring the veg dishes and the gravy boat?"

Candice wondered if she'd really put her foot in it with the marriage question. It was an innocent enquiry. It just seemed to her that if the couple were committed to having a baby, they might want to get married. Everyone was doing it these days, now that they could.

†

"What's next?"

JJ looked at Clare, surprised to be addressed, but Ade and Guido had both disappeared, helping with clearing the plates and remains of the turkey.

"What?" She had been miles away, thinking about the last time she had been out for a meal with Shelley, and finding she couldn't remember either when or where it had been. Was that before or after Shelley had started seeing someone else?

"I mean, food-wise." The actress persisted. "I'm guessing from the cutlery remaining on the table that there's another course."

"Oh, yeah. Well, it will be a flaming pudding."

"You don't like the pudding?"

"Yeah, I do. But not too much, it's very rich."

Clare laughed. "You called it a 'flaming' pudding. I take it that's not meant as an insult."

JJ couldn't help smiling. "No. It gets covered in brandy and set on fire just before they carry it in."

"How quaint."

"So what are Christmas celebrations like in Oz?"

"Nothing like this, obviously. This is like something out of Dickens. Over there it's swimming cossies, and barbies on the beach."

"Barbies? You play with dolls?"

"Barbecues. And cossies are swimming outfits."

They both laughed, and were still laughing when Rita came in, holding the burning pudding at arm's length in front of her. Everyone clapped and cheered.

JJ felt the tears threatening again. It was all too much. Everything here was so perfect. The house, the surroundings, all the trappings of a good old-fashioned family Christmas, with the company of other lesbians. This would have been the best holiday they'd had in years. *Why, Shel? How could you do this to me, now?*

With the ceremonial cake cutting and general hubbub over the wonders of a real Christmas pudding making its dramatic entry, she was able to sniff back the impending waterworks. She dabbed at her eyes with her napkin. She wasn't going to let Shelley's defection spoil this for everyone else here.

Another nudge from Clare who was looking at the plate she'd been handed.

"What's this?"

"It's the hard sauce."

Clare poked the white mound with her knife. "It's not a sauce."

"No, it's more of a spread, really. Made with butter and rum or brandy. Just put a bit of it on the pudding and it will melt in."

Clare did as JJ said and passed the sauce on to her. JJ passed it to Ade.

"You're not having any?"

"I prefer custard on mine."

"Shit. There's custard as well?"

JJ nodded to the other side of the table where Sally was pouring the yellow liquid onto her pudding.

"Damn. Never mind the Queen's speech. I think we should all do an hour's workout after this."

"Nah. Tradition says you have to fall asleep in front of the TV."

"No kidding. I don't think that's going to be a problem."

JJ couldn't believe she was eating anything at all. But she realised that, for all the conflicting emotions running through her, she was in the best place. She hadn't known any of these people two days ago, but they were all showing her nothing but kindness and empathy. She couldn't sit in her room and wallow in her misery. Life went on, with or without her. And without Shelley. She would survive.

†

Guido shooed the women out of the kitchen. "Go see Queen. I wash."

He had just finished stacking the plates in the dishwasher when Felicity came in with her dishes.

"Everyone happy?"

"*Si. No problemo.*"

He turned on the tap to start filling the sink with hot water. Teresa wasn't a messy cook so there weren't a lot of pots to be washed.

Felicity hit him on the arm. "Leave those for now. I'll help you with them. Time for a fag break."

"*Si*. Good idea, old one."

She opened the door and was greeted with a blast of cold air. The snow had mostly stopped, just a few large flakes were floating softly to the ground in a lazy, hypnotic motion. Their footprints from earlier were completely covered and their snow horse now a ghostly shape in the gathering gloom.

Guido stood next to her in the doorway, lit two cigarettes and handed one to her. They stood in companionable silence, enjoying the quiet beauty of the scene, watching the smoke mingling with their exhaled breath.

†

Wil stood by the coffeepot listening to the drips and watching the snow falling.

"Hey, I think it's ready now."

Ade's voice cut into her thoughts.

"You kicked her, didn't you?" she said, without turning around.

"Well, she'd already mentioned it to Gaby just before you sat down. Luckily the ensuing commotion with crackers being pulled created a diversion."

The tray was already set up, so Wil switched off the coffeemaker and removed the full jug to place next to the mugs.

"So when are you going to ask her?"

"When the time's right."

"You've been saying that for two years, at least. I don't know why you didn't pop the question last year, before…"

Wil turned and stared her friend down.

Ade held her hands up and backed off. "You're a stubborn little shit, aren't you? What, are you going to wait until the kid's fifteen?"

"Just take the coffee in. I'll bring the tea."

"Fine, fine, avoid the issue, again," Ade muttered under her breath as she picked up the tray and stalked out.

Wil stood by the door waiting for the kettle to boil. She didn't know why she was putting off asking Gaby to marry her. It wasn't like she thought Gaby would say "no." It felt like they'd been married for years. Ade was right. She'd had many opportunities to ask but had always bottled out at the last minute. In her twenties, marriage hadn't really been a consideration. But she was going to be forty on her next birthday and now they were having a child. She wanted to give her daughter everything she had missed out on as a child. A proper home, a loving environment, two parents who were married—to each other.

She wasn't commitment shy. Gabriella was the love of her life and after last night's re-affirmation; she had no doubts that Gaby felt the same way.

"It's not rocket science, you dope." She rinsed the teapot with boiled water before putting the tealeaves in and filling the pot up. "Just ask her."

†

Sally couldn't fault the food, and the attention to detail was impeccable, but the seating arrangement had been crap. She hadn't wanted to talk to either of the women she was seated between. At first, she'd thought she was going to be lucky and have Felicity Evans next to her, but then she looked at the name card and saw it was the other one, Rose. She might have been able to talk to Mags, who seemed to have cheered up immensely, but Mags only had eyes for Gabriella and was talking to her in a combination of languages somewhere between French, Italian, and English. Which seemed strange, as she was sure both of them spoke English perfectly well.

After the pudding had been consumed, everyone trooped obediently into the lounge with the promise of coffee and tea to follow. Rose, she noticed, disappeared into the off-limits study. Sally had managed to pick up the information during the meal that Felicity had chosen to eat in there with the dogs.

Teresa headed off up the stairs, presumably to have a lie down after being responsible for producing the meal. Gabriella followed more slowly, no doubt also planning to have a rest.

With the dwindling numbers, there was just the slim chance Sally might be able to get Wil Tyler or Ade McPherson on their own. She was pretty sure they weren't going to sit in the lounge watching the Queen's speech.

†

Ade surveyed the guests who all appeared lethargic, even Sally. She rubbed her hands together and made an effort to rouse them.

"So, anyone want to watch the Queen?"

They all shook their heads, apart from Candice who said 'Yes'.

"Majority rules. Sorry, Candice. But it will be shown again later this evening."

"It'll be on YouTube five minutes after the official broadcast," Sally interjected. "The Queen has her own channel."

"Really?" Candice seemed interested.

"Yeah, she's on Twitter as well. Although I doubt she does her own tweets."

Ade opened the cupboard that housed the DVD collection. "Okay, so it's movie time." She pulled out two big handfuls and placed them on the coffee table between the sofas. "Choose."

Mags sat up and started to look through the pile. Ade added some more.

"*Elena Undone*. Yeah, that was good."

"No, please. Not the straight-woman-falls-for-lesbian cliché." Sally picked up a couple of cases. "*Steel Magnolias*, that was a good film."

"Can't stand that Julia Roberts." JJ had opened her eyes.

"But it's not just her. It was a great cast. Shirley MacLaine, Dolly Parton, Olympia Dukakis."

"Speaking of Dukakis, what about *Cloudburst*?"

"Yes, that was great. And it's Canadian too!"

"Hey, look, *Miss Marple*. The Joan Hickson ones, they were the best." JJ had picked up the box set and was reading the info on the back.

Ade watched them scrabbling through the DVD cases. It wasn't the party game she would have planned but it seemed to have perked them all up.

"*Blade Runner, Star Wars, Kill Bill…*" Sally gave Ade a quizzical look.

"Those were Wil's."

"How about an Amy Ransom film? That would be appropriate, wouldn't it?" Candice glanced around at the others.

Clare sighed, "Oh, please! I'm on holiday."

"All right," Ade decided to step in. "We'll put it to the vote. A *Miss Marple* or *Cloudburst*. Hands up for *Cloudburst*."

Mags and Candice, predictably, shot their hands into the air.

"*Miss Marple*."

JJ quickly raised her arm, followed by Clare and Sally.

"*Miss Marple* it is. JJ, you choose one."

She didn't hesitate. "*A Murder is Announced*. That's the one with the two spinsters, Miss Murgatroyd and Miss Hinchcliffe."

"Didn't one of them get killed?"

"Of course. The lesbian always gets it."

"I don't think Agatha intended them to be a couple."

"But that's how they play it in this one. It's never spelled out, just implied."

Ade took the disc from JJ and switched on the TV and DVD player. While the BBC intro played out, Clare helped her move one of the sofas so they could all see the screen comfortably.

Checking that no one wanted more food or drink, Ade and Rita watched the first few minutes of the recording, then slipped out into the hallway.

"That should keep them occupied for a few hours."

"Good thinking, Batman." Rita pecked her on the cheek. "I'm going to see how Guido's doing with the clearing up. What are your plans? And it better not be a nap."

"No such luck. I need to have a business meeting with Wil, if I can track her down."

"She'll be in the study. I heard her tell Rose that would be her last stop once she'd finished the fire rounds."

"Will you join us?"

"Maybe. I'll check on Gaby though when I've finished in the kitchen."

"It's a good thing we came down when we did. I'd hate to think of them stuck here in this weather."

"Yes. But they would have coped. Felicity and Rose and Gaby's parents, they're all very capable."

"What if the baby comes?"

"Well, fat lot of use you'll be for a start." Rita gave her an affectionate peck on the cheek before Ade could protest. "See you later, sweetheart."

Ade watched her move gracefully down the hallway. Was it possible, after twenty years, to fall more in love? It seemed it was. She smiled to herself as she walked the short distance across the hall to the study.

†

Rose was dozing on the sofa with a dog on either side of her when Wil arrived in the study. This room was the last on her checklist of making sure all the fireplaces were stoked up. She'd made several trips to the woodpile already to lay in supplies.

The older woman opened her eyes when Wil came in and made the effort to sit up. Neither of the dogs stirred.

"You don't need to move, Rose. I'm just checking on the fire."

"I said I'd help with the washing up. They'll be finished by now and cursing my name." She got to her feet. Raffi did raise his head, no doubt annoyed that she'd left his side exposed to the air.

"Do they need to go out to do their business?"

"No. I tried to get them to go. But you'd be amazed how long they can hold it in when they put their minds to it."

"I'll come and help with the dishes as well."

"No, you won't. You've been running around all day. Just sit down for a bit. We can manage." Rose gave her a quick hug and a peck on the cheek before leaving the room.

Wil put another log on the fire and sat on the hearth staring into the flames. A moment of calm. So far the day hadn't proved too much of a disaster. The unexpected snowfall had helped to lighten the mood, in spite of Shelley's early morning defection, and the lack of communication with the outside world. Wil wondered what would have happened if there hadn't been any snow. Would JJ have wanted to go after Shelley? As it was, she was trapped here with no way of knowing where Shelley had gone. Would Wil even now be driving an increasingly frantic JJ around Brighton trying to find her girlfriend? Ex-girlfriend now. Christmas Day, what a shitty time to end a relationship. Couldn't she have waited until the start of the New Year, at least?

She was startled out of her musings when Ade came in. "They're all settled in, watching a *Miss Marple* of all things."

"Comfort viewing, I guess."

"I'm not sure about that. I think it's a bit macabre. Here we are, trapped in a country house. Ideal set up for a murder mystery."

"Well, let's hope it doesn't come to that. We've enough problems for now, keeping everyone warm and hoping the power lines don't go down."

"And hoping Gaby doesn't go into labour."

"I don't even want to think about that."

Ade helped herself to a glass of whisky. "Do you want anything?"

Wil shook her head.

"Right, down to business."

"Can't it wait until tomorrow?" Wil moved from the hearth and flopped down on the sofa in the space between the two dogs. She stroked each of them behind their ears. Raffi snuffled contentedly in his sleep, and Daisy raised her head to look at Wil and then settled down again.

Ade stretched her legs out in front of her as she seated herself in the chair opposite. "I may not have another chance to get you on your own, so this is it. The main thing is a revamp for the website. It's looking dated. If Gaby's not up to it, I'll try and take some photos tomorrow. The snow scenes will look great. Has she got any recent summer ones in her portfolio?"

"Yes. I know she took some while everything was in bloom."

"Okay, that's good. Are you going ahead with creating an adventure trail in the woods? You know, zip-line, obstacle course, that kind of thing?"

"We've talked about it, but I think now that we might just be creating problems for ourselves. If guests use it unsupervised, which they will, what happens when someone gets injured?"

"Anything else new?"

"We've got a yoga instructor lined up. She's ready to start in January. And Mark's also been in touch with a friend of his who teaches Tai Chi."

"So, you've gone from swinging through the trees to old lady activities."

"Tai Chi is a martial art and yoga is very good for you. People who come here generally just want to relax. The more energetic ones do horse riding or go for runs. Plus we're looking at water aerobics classes in the pool."

"Might as well just advertise it as a health farm."

"Why not? Lesbians can be healthy, too."

Ade knocked back the last of her whisky. "Sure. Well, I guess it's a start."

The door opened and Rita came in carrying a tray. "Coffee, anyone?"

Wil smiled at her. "You're an angel."

Setting the tray down carefully, Rita gave her a penetrating look. "Good thing for you Gaby's resting. I wouldn't want to be in your shoes if she were to come in and see the dogs on the furniture."

"It's their Christmas treat," Wil protested.

"I should think Felicity's already spoiled them with hearty helpings of turkey."

"Have you looked in on the guests?" Ade asked, deflecting any further recriminations.

"Yes. JJ and Clare are watching the film; at least they still have their eyes open. Sally's reading a book and making notes. The other two are asleep." Rita sat down on the hearth and poured out the coffee.

"What about the oldies?" Wil liked to keep track of everyone.

"Guido managed to find a pair of ski boots that fit, so he's gone down to the stables with the other two to check on the horses."

"Let's hope T doesn't find out. It's quite a climb back up the hill on skis. She'll have a fit."

"He's more likely to die from lung cancer than a heart attack. Anyway, Wil, I was thinking…"

"I've told you before, that's dangerous." Ade grinned at her over her coffee mug.

"I'll deal with you later. I was thinking we should provide hot water bottles for the guests tonight. Have we got enough?"

"Yes, I think so. We had a cold spell a few years ago when we had to go out and buy some." Wil sipped her coffee. Being in this room was her security blanket. Surrounded now by the gentle snuffles of the sleeping dogs and her two best friends, she could feel her fears for the future seeping away.

†

Sally didn't think anyone would notice if she left the room. JJ and Clare seemed engrossed in the drama on screen. Candice and Mags were definitely asleep, curled into each other.

She marked the place in the book with a piece of wrapping paper that had been missed in the clear up after the present-opening session before lunch. Book seven was her favourite of the whole Amy Ransom series. She'd just had the realisation that it contained autobiographical hints. In all the books there was usually a steamy sex scene involving Amy and whichever character turned out to be the villain. Amy Ransom was always attracted to the dark side. In book seven, she encounters Shay Finch again and their meeting is even more intense than in book four where they first met. The book was dedicated to Clare and had been written after the author's fling with the actress.

It would take some time to research, but Sally thought there would probably be clues in all the books. However, in order to winkle them out, she needed more facts about Kim's life. The Wikipedia entry was a stub. No one had updated it since its appearance on the site in 2006. When she mentioned this to Thelma, the old woman had looked at her blankly. Sally told her the page needed a complete list of Kim Russell's books with links to the films. There was more documentation online about the movies than the books. Thelma hadn't even been aware that there was a whole series of Amy Ransom fan fiction. Or that there were numerous Facebook groups and fake Twitter accounts with thousands of followers.

Sally wanted to be recognised as Kim Russell's official biographer, which was why she had approached the old woman in the first place. Thelma had told her that to gain access to more personal information, she would have to talk to the executors of Kim's estate, and that meant talking to Wil Tyler and Ade McPherson.

Sally stood outside the study door. The sound of voices told her that they were in there. Taking a deep breath, she knocked. After what seemed like an age, the door opened and she was faced with the cute redhead. Well, better her than the imposing figure of Ade's partner, Rita.

"Um, hi, sorry to bother you. I was wondering if there are any Cary Fontaine books around." Sally hadn't managed to come up with a better excuse for disturbing the owner of the house.

Wil Tyler folded her arms across her chest. What was she protecting, for God's sake? It was fifteen years since the author had died.

"Sorry, no."

"Oh. I just thought, since you have all the Amy ones, first editions and all…"

"Kim destroyed them herself."

"Really." Now this was interesting. "Why would she do that?"

If Wil had been going to answer she was prevented from doing so by the appearance of the formidable Rita at her side.

"Is there a problem?" she asked quietly. "Would you like more tea or coffee?"

Rita somehow made the offer sound menacing. Sally backed away. "No, everything's fine, thanks. See you later." Walking slowly across the hall, she shook her head. Somehow, in the next two days, she needed to get someone here to talk.

†

"What was all that about?" Ade asked after Rita shut the door and the two of them resumed their seats.

"Nosy cow! What do you know about her, Wil?" Rita pulled the poker out of the log basket.

"Nothing, apart from her name. We don't do background checks on our guests."

"Well, maybe you should. I'd Google her if the Wi-Fi was working. She's up to something." Rita gave the burning log a stir, sending sparks up the chimney.

"How do you know that? She may have just wanted company over Christmas. Not much fun on your own."

"I've seen ten-year-olds who can lie better than her. Believe me, she has another agenda."

"I thought she was just after Clare." Ade poured herself a cup of coffee.

"Clare can handle herself. Anyway, Wil, what about your little white lie? I know you have both Cary Fontaine books."

Ade glanced over at her young friend. She was too far away to give her wife a discreet kick and she was still holding the poker at a threatening angle. Wil had closed her eyes and Ade thought maybe she wasn't going to answer Rita's question. But she quickly opened them again.

"It wasn't a good time, not for either of us. Kim had stopped writing. After my mother's death. AR5 was in the editing stage and she managed to finish it for publication. Then she abandoned Amy, abandoned everything."

Ade knew what she was struggling with. She had been here. That morning when Wil turned up at the house after running away from her foster home, away from the life she'd been forced into with her mother's murder. Ade hadn't known the whole story at the time. Only years later, soon after Wil started at university, had she managed to get Wil to talk about it.

"I'm sorry, hon." Rita had realised her mistake too late. Ade gave her a reassuring smile.

Wil stroked Daisy's head and looked up at them both. "The Cary Fontaine stories were much darker than anything she'd ever written. I haven't been able to read either of the books all the way through. I wish they'd never been published and, thankfully, they're now out of print." She stood abruptly. "I'll ferret out the extra hot water bottles. See you guys later."

Rita waited until the door closed behind her before turning to Ade. "I really put my foot in it, didn't I? But I had no idea she connects her mother with those books. And it's been, what, twenty-five years almost since it happened."

"I don't think it's something you ever forget. Even though she wasn't close to her mother, she was at a very vulnerable stage in her life. Who'd want to be a teenager again?" Ade placed her coffee mug on the tray and got to her feet slowly. Age was catching up with her as she felt a twinge in her lower back. Just sitting for a short time made everything stiffen up. She picked up the tray. "I'll go and check on the guests. You relax, sweetheart."

Rita smiled at her and seated herself in the chair Ade had recently abandoned. "Too right. I'm just going to close my eyes for a bit."

When Ade looked back before quietly closing the door, Rita was already asleep.

# Chapter Five

## Christmas Evening

Wil set the glass of water on the bedside table and looked down at the sleeping woman. Her black hair was spread across the pillow and she looked as fresh faced as when they first met, flushed with youth, her beauty enhanced by impending motherhood.

"Are you awake?" she asked softly, reaching out to brush a stray strand away from Gaby's mouth.

"*Si, cara.*" Her eyelids fluttered open, brown eyes clouded with sleep.

"I've brought you some water."

"*Grazie.*"

Wil sat down on the bed. She reached over and took one of Gaby's hands in hers. It was warm, even though the room was cold.

"I want to ask you something."

"I know." Gaby's eyes had cleared; the deep brown pools gazed up at her.

Wil swallowed. Those eyes had captured her from the first moment she'd seen Gaby. "The thing is, I was thinking, we should get married. If you want to, that is."

"Of course. I was just waiting."

"Waiting for me to ask?"

"No. Waiting for you to be ready."

"Funny. That's just what your mother said." Wil couldn't meet her eyes.

"You talked to mama first?"

"*Si.* I know it's not necessary nowadays, but I wanted to make sure your parents were happy with the idea. I mean Guido's not much of a churchgoer, but your mum is and well, you know, the Catholic Church isn't too thrilled about gay people getting married."

Gaby reached up with her free hand and stroked the side of her face. "You are too sweet. Mama adores you, they both do. And mama already has the wedding planned, so don't think you're getting out of it now."

Without letting go of Gaby's hand, Wil reached into the drawer of the bedside table. She pulled out a small box and presented it to her lover. "I don't want to get out of it, ever. I bought this a year ago. Hope it still fits."

Gaby moved slowly into a sitting position, releasing Wil's hand. She opened the box and looked at the ring nestled inside. "*Bellissima!*"

Wil took the box from her. The ring slipped easily onto Gaby's finger. "Gabriella Brunetti, will you do me the honour of becoming my wife?"

"*Si, si!*" Tears were shining in the corners of her eyes as she moved her gaze from the ring to Wil's face. "I love you so much," she whispered as she reached out to bring Wil's head closer. When their lips met, Wil felt the full force of Gaby's passion and melted into her embrace.

†

"*Quando?*" Guido warmed his hands on the electric room heater.

"Soon. Before christening, I hope." Teresa was wrapped in a bath towel, still glowing from the warmth of her bath.

He smiled to himself. His wife would want things done in the right order. Marriage first. When their daughter first told them she was gay, they had initially struggled with the concept, wondering what they had done wrong. But the day she brought Wil Tyler home, all their worries had vanished. The quiet, seemingly withdrawn young woman brought out a spark in Gaby they hadn't seen before.

Gaby's decision to follow her new love, and move permanently to England, had been a blow. But when they saw the home she had come to set in the lush green countryside, that too had settled any concerns. Their daughter thrived on the work of renovating the old manor house to create a peaceful haven for prospective guests. And the more they saw of Wil and her dedication to the project, and to making Gaby happy, they were content with their daughter's choice of partner.

Guido knew some of Wil's history from talking to Felicity. With that knowledge he had been able to understand why it was taking Wil so long to make the final step to a lifelong commitment. Teresa had been remarkably patient, too. She said the time would come when Wil was ready.

"*Buon.* Now, Felicity want revenge. Setting up bridge table in study." He rubbed his hands together.

Teresa smiled sweetly at him. The smile that fooled their opponents into thinking they had a chance of winning. "We have wedding to pay for now. Easy pickings."

153

Guido laughed. This was an expression Felicity had used the first time they played, thinking simple Italian farmers would be ignorant of the finer points of the game when she suggested they play for money. Easy pickings, indeed, only not the way the horsewoman had envisaged.

†

The day was going pretty much to plan, Ade thought. The guests were all in the lounge either watching the film or dozing. Wil had gone up to talk to Teresa. Rita was asleep in the study. Ade had emptied the dishwasher and started sorting out the hot water bottles that Wil had left on the table when Felicity and Rose reappeared, carrying a card table between them.

"You're not..." she didn't get to finish before Felicity interrupted her.

"Yes, we are. We have some money to recoup."

"Where are you going to play?"

"The study, of course."

"Rita's sleeping in there."

"Not any more." Rita appeared in the doorway. "I let the dogs out and they've both done their business. They were pretty quick about it and didn't want to hang around outside."

"Well, they're not as young as they were," Rose said. "I've brought some more of their food up." She put down her end of the table and removed her knapsack.

Rita took it from her. "Good. I was going to start on the supper prep anyway."

"It's a never-ending food-fest." Ade protested. "Is anyone really going to want to eat again today?"

"That's the whole point of Christmas Day," Felicity said, nudging the table into the back of Rose's leg.

"Don't let T hear you say that. She thinks it has something to do with the birth of Christ. She was disappointed she couldn't get to church this morning." Ade moved over to the sink to fill the kettle. "Anyone for a brew?"

"Ooh, yes please. I could murder a nice cup of tea." Rose smiled at her sweetly.

"I'll murder you if you don't pick up your end." Felicity nudged her leg again.

"Here. I'll take the table." Ade grabbed it from Felicity. "You two get your coats off. And Gaby will kill the pair of you if you carry on through the house with your boots on."

Rita laughed. "She's right. And I'll make the tea so I can get all of you out of the kitchen."

†

Clare watched the *Miss Marple* film with a detached professional interest. She had seen it before and knew how it ended, but with such a fine cast of British actors, it was always a joy to watch. Sally's departure hadn't gone unnoticed, and from her look of disappointment when she returned, Clare deduced that it wasn't necessarily a bathroom break. More likely Sally was on the prowl to get Wil on her own.

Clare could sympathise with her problem. The writer was hoping to get the inside story to validate her status as official biographer. But coming here, disguised as a guest, was an underhanded way of doing it. Why hadn't she just made an appointment? Clare doubted Wil was in the right frame of mind to talk to Sally at this time. Her partner was about to give birth and she was concerned with making sure all the guests had what they needed. Being snowbound until the drive could be cleared was likely to be a big worry for Wil as well. No communication with the outside world. The setting was perfect for an Agatha Christie story. Hopefully there wouldn't be any sinister turn of events.

Knowing what she did now of Sally's real reason for being here, Clare's dilemma was whether or not she should let Wil know. Or would that just be adding to Wil's current problems?

Clare looked around as the film ended. Candice and Mags were still snoozing.

"Anyone fancy a swim?"

JJ put the remote for the DVD player back on the table. "Can we even get to the pool building?"

Clare stood and went over to the window. It was now dark but there was no more snow falling. "If we wear boots, I would think we can make a path. I just feel I need some exercise without getting too cold."

"The pool's heated, I guess."

"Yes, it's like a warm bath. What about you, Sally?"

The writer looked up from her notebook. "I didn't bring a swimming costume."

"Hey, we're all women. Who needs cossies?"

Candice had woken up and was looking at her wide-eyed. "Are you suggesting a skinny dip?"

"Sure, why not? Our hosts have buggered off. We need to make our own entertainment."

Mags was awake too. "I'm in."

"All right!" Clare looked at the group. "So, everyone tog up with hats, coats, boots. No point risking hypothermia before we get there. Last one in the pool is a *pommy bludger*!"

She laughed to herself as she headed out of the room, followed by sounds of the others scrambling to their feet and a muttered: "Is a what?"

†

A wave of water caught her in the face. JJ screamed and splashed her attacker back. What started as a playful romp had turned into a full-on water fight. Earlier in the day, she really couldn't have imagined she would be having this much fun. The sight of so many boobs bobbing around in the water easily drove away her depression.

Clare had led the way through the snow to the chalet. They all followed in her footsteps creating, as she'd said, a path. Once inside, garments had been hastily cast off in the rush not to be last in the pool. The Australian actress was the first to strip completely and entered the water with a perfect dive, hardly causing a ripple in the surface.

JJ stood with her mouth open. The woman was drop-dead gorgeous with her clothes on. With them off, she was a goddess in the flesh. A perfect all over tan, golden hair everywhere.

Sally nudged her. "Never mind a swim, I'll need a cold shower after this." She leapt into the pool in a much less elegant manner, feet first.

Diving under the water to evade the next onslaught, JJ wrapped her arms around the first leg she found and pulled its owner under. After much thrashing around they both surfaced and JJ was faced with a spluttering and enraged Clare. JJ moved quickly to evade her long reach and swam to the other end of the pool where Candice was resting peacefully against the side, just moving her legs back and forth.

"Not joining in, Candy?"

"Candice, unless you want to be called Jane."

"Oh, yeah, sorry." Belatedly, JJ recalled the conversation at the lunch table.

"And, no. I'm not much of a swimmer. I'll paddle about here in the shallow end."

"Marguerite's enjoying herself," JJ carefully enunciated the other woman's full name.

Candice grinned at her. "Yes, she is. And she doesn't mind being called Mags."

A change in Candice's expression warned JJ a fraction too late that she had been caught. She closed her mouth just in time as she was dragged under the water.

† 

Seeing Mags enjoying herself made this whole trip worthwhile, Candice thought, as she regained peace at her end of the pool when Clare forcibly took JJ back to the melee in the war zone.

She had been the last to get into the pool, feeling self-conscious when she had undressed, surrounded by the toned bodies of the other women. Clare translated "pommy bludger" as "English lay-about," and Candice laughingly told her it was a terrible insult. A *bludger* she might be, but being Canadian with Irish heritage, she objected to being called a *pommy*.

Maybe they should have done this yesterday. As an icebreaker for a group it had its merits. Maybe then Shelley wouldn't have left. But it seemed she'd had it all planned out anyway. Poor JJ. She seemed nice enough. But what did anyone know about other people's relationships? She'd seen friends break up over seemingly trivial matters. Candice looked down the length of the pool again and smiled at her partner's antics. She knew that whatever difficulties they faced, they would overcome them together. Mags was worth it. Their shared life together was worth it.

†

Ade finished laying out the supper table as per Rita's instructions. She thought the arrangements were over the top. The comatose state she'd last seen the guests in, they weren't likely to want another morsel to eat. Still, Rita was determined to do everything the way she knew Gaby would want it done. Having taken charge of the kitchen for the day, she wouldn't let her young friend down.

Time to look for the other youngster. Wil had been in a strange mood and it wouldn't hurt to check she was okay.

Rita came in with a covered plate.

"What's on there?"

"Nothing you would like."

"Are you sure? Let me see."

"Hands off." She placed it on the table and looked around. "Good job, sweetie. Now, would you mind just checking on the oldies? See if they want anything?"

"If they're in the middle of a rubber, they won't be interested."

"Well, just ask. I don't want any of them complaining they've been neglected."

"I'm feeling neglected."

Rita turned to her and put her hands on her waist, pulling her close. "Give me a kiss, then."

Ade complied and felt a surge of warmth as their lips met, savouring the heady scents of her wife's skin mixed with the spicy aromas from the kitchen.

Rita pulled back and smiled at her. "Later, I promise."

"I'm holding you to that."

Rita walked away from her, giving a provocative sway to her hips as she returned to the kitchen. Such a tease. Ade licked her lips, relishing the thought of their later encounter.

No one looked up when she entered the study. Daisy was lying on the floor in front of the fire and thumped her tail in brief recognition of her presence. Raffi had taken full possession of the sofa and didn't move.

Ade could see that the card players were in the middle of a hand and even Rose, who was dummy, was concentrating hard. The hand played out with Felicity managing to get the requisite number of tricks. Guido muttered something under his breath.

Ade coughed and they all turned to look at her. "Sorry to bother you, folks. Rita wants to know if you need anything else to eat or drink. The buffet will be ready in about half an hour."

They all shook their heads. Rose was shuffling the pack.

"Anyone seen Wil?"

Teresa looked up at her and smiled broadly. "She and Gaby, they are engaged now, I think."

"Oh, good. I won't have to bang her head against the wall again. That's great news."

Ade left them to their game and walked across the hall. The day was ending better than it had started. With everyone else in the house accounted for, she opened the door to the lounge and stood transfixed on the threshold. It was empty, of people anyway. What the fuck? Were they playing Hide and Seek or Sardines? She calmed herself down. They had probably just gone to their rooms to freshen up before the buffet.

She walked back to the kitchen.

"That's weird. The guests have all disappeared. I mean to lose one may be regarded as a misfortune..."

"...To lose all smacks of carelessness." Rita finished misquoting the famous line from *The Importance of Being Earnest*. "I heard some commotion in the hallway a little while ago. They may have gone outside."

"To play in the snow? They're all grownups, for fuck's sake."

"The fresh air will do them good since they've been sitting around all afternoon."

Ade went out and opened the back door. It had stopped snowing and it was a clear night with the stars emphasising the blackness of the sky. A perfect night for stargazing. The snowy expanse of the lawn was pristine with just a single track of footprints leading to the chalet. She checked inside the door and sure enough the key for the swimming pool was missing.

She returned to the kitchen. "Can you believe it? They've gone for a swim."

Rita looked up from the cheese board she was garnishing. "Well, could you get them back in? Everything will be ready soon, and they'll all want to get showered and changed, I should think."

"Sure, if I can find some boots to fit. Someone's taken mine."

"Guido's should fit you. Go on. I can't keep the sausage rolls hot indefinitely."

The sight that met her eyes when she entered the swimming pool area was something she could never have dreamt. Five naked women cavorting in the water. She leant against the doorframe and waited for them to notice her.

Clare was first and jumped up exposing her magnificent torso, "Hey, McPherson. Come on in!"

Ade shook her head. "You're all nuts." She went to the cupboard and pulled out five towels. "Get your lovely butts dried and dressed. Rita's been slaving over a hot stove and you seriously don't want to annoy her by letting anything get cold."

She held out the towels, averting her eyes as the women clambered out of the pool one by one. Of course the reflection in the windows gave her a good view of their bodies as they shuffled around, drying themselves off, and looking for the clothes that had obviously been discarded in a hurry.

Ushering them out into the cold night, Ade locked the door of the chalet and set off after them. Clare waited for her, letting the others get ahead.

"Could I have a word?"

"Sure. Here, or do you want to wait until we get inside?"

Clare glanced up the path. "Here's okay. I just thought I should let you know that Sally's planning on writing Kim's biography. That's why she's here. She wants to talk to you and Wil particularly. She's already tried it on with me."

Ade started up the path and Clare followed. "Damn, Rita was right, again. She suspected Sally was up to something."

"It's down to you and Wil, of course. But maybe you should just talk to her."

They reached the back door of the house. The others had already shed their boots and coats. Ade replaced the chalet key on its hook.

"I'll speak to Wil, but not tonight. She's just got engaged."

"Strewth! I thought they were already married. You and Rita are, aren't you?"

"Yes. Last year. But we'd already done the civil partnership, so it was just a matter of filling in a form. Wil doesn't know what she's in for. Teresa will have planned a whole white wedding."

"I might have to stick around to see that."

Ade punched her arm. "Go on and get showered. Thanks for letting me know about Sally. We'll talk again in the morning."

†

The pool activity had been fun and Sally couldn't believe she'd actually worked up an appetite. She stood at the buffet table looking at the vast array of food. A few hours earlier she would have said no to eating anything ever again.

But it was all beautifully presented, and she did feel a few pangs of hunger now. She helped herself to a sausage roll and some salad. Best to leave room for cheese, there was such a fine selection.

A burst of laughter from the doorway made her look round. JJ was holding onto Clare's arm, pointing up to the top of the doorframe, which had a sprig of mistletoe pinned to it. Sally was sure it hadn't been there earlier in the day.

"So, if I stand here, I have to kiss you?" Clare sounded incredulous.

"Yes, and you're in for seven years bad luck if you don't." JJ puckered up her lips.

This was a different person from the abandoned lover Sally had brought breakfast to that morning. She watched with envy as Clare complied, saying, "Well, I don't need that."

She wasn't sure how long they would have remained lip-locked if Candice and Mags hadn't arrived with Candice saying loudly, "Move out of the way and we'll show you how to do it properly."

Clare and JJ broke apart and came into the room. They applauded when the Canadian couple finished their ceremonial kiss.

JJ noticed her standing on her own. "Hey, Sally, come over here and stand under the mistletoe. You get to kiss the next person who comes in."

"No thanks. With my luck it will be Signor Brunetti."

"Well, I'm sure he wouldn't mind."

"Wow, this is an amazing spread." Candice had moved over to the buffet table.

Sally left them all picking their way through the food and carried her plate into the lounge. Ade was there, stoking up the fire.

"Ah, Sally. Good. I'd like a word with you."

"The skinny dip wasn't my idea."

"Not about that. I understand you're here because you want to write a biography of Kim, am I right?"

"Um, yes." Sally put her plate on the table, any desire for food deserting her.

"Okay. So, why not just contact us before coming here? This is rather an expensive way of finding out that we might not be happy with the idea." The tall woman loomed over her, arms folded across her chest.

"I talked to the old... Thelma Barton."

"And did Thelma think we would want to talk to you?"

"She thought it was doubtful."

"But you came anyway."

"Well, I wanted to see the place. It's also an important part of Kim's story. And it seemed like it might be a good opportunity to talk to people who were close to her. Bit of a bonus, Clare turning up." The light dawned. "Oh, Clare told you, didn't she?"

"Yes, and I'm glad she did." Ade backed off slightly and put her hands in her pockets, a much less threatening stance. "Look, your timing is shit. Which I'm sure you've probably realised by now." She sighed heavily. "But there's no point you sneaking around. Might as well get it out in the open. I will speak to Wil in the morning. If she's amenable, and there's no guarantee she will be, then we'll find a time to talk to you."

"Great. Thanks. I appreciate it."

165

Ade moved closer again and this time she did look menacing. "If we weren't snowed in, you would be on the first fucking train back to London, make no mistake. Wil doesn't need this. Not now. Not ever."

Before Sally could react, the door opened and the other guests arrived. Ade switched smoothly into charming host mode.

"Please help yourselves to whatever you want to drink. Wine, juice, water, all here on the sideboard. We'll be serving coffee for anyone who wants it later. And stuff yourselves stupid, because there are lively party games with prizes afterwards."

With one last meaning-filled glance her way, Ade left the room. *Party games and prizes?* Sally didn't feel like partying. The euphoria from the impromptu splash around in the pool had dissipated in the face of Ade's undisguised anger.

"Hey, Sal, aren't you going to eat this?"

She turned back to the others who were now seated and munching away, plates stacked high with food from the buffet. They all looked remarkably cheerful, rosy-cheeked from their recent showers and mistletoe encounters. It was JJ who had called out to her, now seemingly back to her naturally buoyant self. Sally didn't think it would last when she found herself back in her room, alone. Although sitting close to Clare with their knees touching, would she be alone?

Sally sat down in the armchair and forced a smile. "I'm not really hungry."

"Come on, it's Christmas. You can work off all the calories shoveling out the driveway tomorrow."

This statement didn't do anything to lift Sally's mood, with Ade's threat hanging in the air. If the drive got cleared, she figured she wouldn't be here by this time tomorrow.

†

Clare watched Sally over the rim of her glass of champagne. Sally had been withdrawn all evening and she couldn't shake off a guilty feeling that she was responsible.

Teaming up with JJ for the first game, they had won easily. Candice and Mags didn't really get to grips with the concept of the Railway Riot. It was probably a better game if more people took part and Ade had asked them to hand in their phones so they couldn't cheat.

Players were given a ticket with a train station name on it and had to search for hidden cards placed randomly around the house to find that name. This card gave them the name of the next station they had to find. There were twelve cards, so it took a fair bit of running about to locate them in an effort to be the first team to reach the final destination. Clare figured out that the reason Ade didn't want them using their phones was so they couldn't just photograph each card to minimise the need to run back and forth. It took them ages to find the card stuck inside a lampshade in the dining room.

The next game wasn't quite so demanding physically. The teams each received a full copy of the previous week's *Sunday Times* newspaper. They were given cards with a headline written on it and had to search through the paper to find it. Once found, they gave their card to Ade and received another one. The trick was to quickly figure out which section of the paper the headline came from. The team that found all fourteen headlines first was the winner. Clare invited Sally to join them for the game, but she wasn't much help.

The prizes were bottles of champagne. Even with sharing, they were all going to be well sozzled before bedtime. JJ had stuck to Clare like glue since the mistletoe kiss. She'd been happy to play along for the evening, but that was as far as it was going to go. She wasn't going to sleep with JJ just because she felt sorry for her.

Sally was another matter. She was attracted to her, but the writer's intense interest in Kim was holding Clare back from making any moves. If Sally was hoping for a kiss-and-tell session, it wasn't going to happen. That wasn't her style, and it would be a betrayal of the woman Clare had loved. Even after all this time, Kim still featured in many of her dreams. Dreams she often didn't want to wake up from.

Clare had been twenty-five when she met Kim, an age when she thought she was in control of her destiny but was, in fact, naive in so many ways. Her happy notion of love 'em and leave 'em came crashing down when Kim returned home. Why did Clare let her get away? She knew there was someone else at home for Kim. Knowing what she did now, Clare should have got on the first plane to England. She should have fought for their chance of happiness together. But maybe that was just a pipe dream. Clare hadn't been aware of Kim's drinking problem until she talked with Wil. And Kim was dead by then.

Such morbid thoughts were interrupted as Ade came back into the room carrying a flip-chart stand. "You thought it was over. Wrong. It's never over until the fat lady sings."

"That would be me," Candice piped up.

Clare smiled at her. "Generously proportioned, I would say."

"Yes, nothing wrong with a good handful." JJ added.

"Now, ladies, let's keep it clean." Ade set up the stand where they could all see it.

"Where's the fun in that?" Sally spoke for the first time in ages.

Ade ignored her and handed around different coloured marker pens. "I guess you're all familiar with Pictionary."

There was a collective groan.

"Come on, it can be fun. I think the teams should split up for this one. Rita's joining us so we can have three. How about JJ with Candice, Mags and Clare, Sally and Rita? Everyone okay with that?"

Rita had come into the room. "Bad luck, Sally. I'm rubbish at this."

Clare switched places with Candice and Rita pulled up the desk chair to sit by Sally. They all looked expectantly at Ade. She held out the Pictionary box of cards and told Candice, who was nearest to her, to pick one.

†

Wil untangled herself from under the duvet. The hours spent snuggling with Gaby, occasionally feeling the baby move, had been blissful. Just what she needed to recharge her batteries. And now they were officially engaged, it was as if a weight she hadn't realised she'd been carrying suddenly melted away. They had talked for a while, softly, exchanging kisses and caresses. She didn't want to leave this heavenly womb-like state, but Gaby had fallen asleep and Wil needed to see what was happening downstairs.

When she glanced at her watch she was surprised to see how much time had passed. Giving her face a quick splash, and a rake through her short hair with her fingers, she was ready to find out how they had all coped without her.

The dining room and kitchen were both tidy. But the pile of hot water bottles on the table reminded her they would need filling before everyone retired to bed for the night.

She looked in the study next. The dogs didn't seem to have moved since she'd last been there. Felicity had the dummy hand and winked at her. Teresa had no doubt told them about the engagement. Wil backed out quietly and walked across to the lounge.

A burst of laughter greeted her. Rita was standing next to the flip chart, which had a drawing of something that looked like the dildo Gaby had thrown in her lap the other day.

"May I remind you of the category," Rita said tartly.

"No, you can't. You're not allowed to speak." Ade was standing apart from the group, looking officious, holding a notepad.

Mags put her hand up and bounced in her seat. "I know, I know. It's Florida."

"Well done. Points for your team. Your turn, Candice."

Rita saw Wil and came over to give her a hug. "Congratulations, sweetheart," she whispered in her ear. "There's plenty of food left from the buffet if you're hungry."

"Thanks. I'll pick at something while I'm filling the hot water bottles."

"Hey, Wil. Congratulations!" Clare called out.

The other guests turned to her. "Congratulations for what?" asked Candice, who had stood up to take her place by the flip chart.

"Gaby and I are now engaged."

"Oh, wow! When's the wedding?" Candice beamed at her.

"We haven't set a date. But we will, after the baby is born." She gave them a big smile. "I'll leave you to it. I understand you've left me some supper."

Wil walked back down the hall to the kitchen. The feeling of lightness was still with her and she wondered why she hadn't asked Gaby to marry her a long time ago.

# Chapter Six

## Boxing Day

Sleep hadn't come easily. Sally didn't think it was anything to do with the amount of champagne she had drunk the night before. She had the uneasy feeling that Clare was avoiding her, as if she now had some communicable disease. Well, she would know soon enough if Wil Tyler would talk to her, that is, if her guard dog would let her.

The enforced digital detox wasn't something she would want to experience for any length of time. It had only been two days but she now had a long list of things to Google once she was able to get back online. She could only go so far with the notes she'd made about the house and the surroundings. Other sources of information, once the snow melted, would be the villagers. There would be people who remembered Kim Russell's arrival. Talking to people who knew her uncle might give her useful leads to other members of the horse-and-country set. Following up on Clare's advice, she had found Grace Green's father listed in *Who's Who*, an outdated version of which had been on the bookshelf in the lounge. He was Sir Antony Coombes, a minor baronet. Although there had been a second marriage, the two boys weren't his, so he had left his estate to his daughter. Grace, as well as being a "national treasure" as far as broadcasting was concerned, was also a wealthy woman.

It stood to reason that the people at Winterbourne House wanted to protect Kim's memory. Grace's autobiography would have made for unpleasant reading. Sally's impetus for wanting to pursue a biography of the writer had stemmed from the angry reaction of fans to GG's book. A dead person couldn't defend herself. But the people who had known her best, the people here, could. If Sally could only get them to talk to her.

†

The sun was streaming through the window when Wil woke. Bathed in sunlight, she felt refreshed from a good night's sleep. Turning over, she realised Gaby's side of the bed was empty. She rolled into the warm space left by her partner's body. Noises from the bathroom indicated that Gaby was showering. Breathing in the lingering scents, she wanted to stay in this cosy cocoon but other noises from the house were filtering through.

Rita and Ade were obviously up and about with the clatter of plates coming from the kitchenette. She'd left most of the work to them the previous day and today she would do her share and more. It wasn't fair on Rita as this was part of her two-week Christmas holiday, a much-needed break from her full-time and demanding job as a schools inspector.

Gaby emerged from the bathroom, towels draped over her head and around her body. Wil summoned up the energy to get out of bed.

"Christ, it's cold!" she cried out as soon as her feet hit the floor. The sunshine had lulled her into a false impression.

Gaby opened the large bath towel and beckoned her over with a tilt of her head and a huge smile. She moved in as close as she could get with the protruding belly between them and kissed her. They stayed glued together for several minutes. Only a sharp movement from the baby separated them.

"Someone else is awake." Wil pulled away reluctantly. "Best get on with the day. *Te amore!*"

"*Si. Ditto. Mia fidanzata ha.*"

"*Fidanzata ha.*" Wil drew the words out. They sounded better than just fiancée, she thought. But Italian was still the language of love to her mind.

Gaby moved away from her to the dressing table to dry her hair and Wil went into the bathroom to have a quick shower.

When she emerged into the kitchenette ten minutes later, washed and dressed, Gaby was seated at the table with Rita, hands wrapped around a mug of tea; something herbal by the look of it. Ade was standing by the toaster.

"Morning, sleepyhead. Thought I was going to have to come in and shake you out."

Wil helped herself to coffee. "It's only half eight. With all the champagne you were giving away last night, I shouldn't think any of the guests will be up yet."

"And that's where you're wrong, again. I saw Clare heading out to the chalet. At least she was by herself this time." Ade placed the toast on a plate and put it in the middle of the table.

"What does it matter, if anyone wants to join her."

"Oh, yeah. You missed the mass skinny-dip."

Wil choked on the coffee she was swallowing.

"I thought we'd lost all the guests, not just one, yesterday afternoon." Ade described the scene she'd witnessed, the pool heaving with naked bodies. "I wish I'd had a camera with me."

"Yes, that would be a great draw if you put it on the website." Wil picked up a slice of toast and started to butter it. Glancing up she just caught the look passing between her two friends. "What? Is there something I should know?"

Ade grimaced. "It can wait until after breakfast."

Wil put the toast down. "No, it can't. You have to tell me now."

"Okay. Well, it seems that Rita was right, as usual, about Sally Hunter. Clare tipped me off and I had words with her." Ade reached over and placed a hand on hers. "She's a writer and she wants to do a biography of Kim. That's why she's here, hoping to get the inside story. Not just from you, but me, and probably Felicity as well. She's already tried Clare."

"*Puttana!*" Gaby rarely swore but the word shot out forcefully.

"What did you say to her?"

"I told her that if we weren't snowed in she'd be on the first train back to London. However, the alternative, as we are stuck here, is to talk to her."

"I don't want…"

"I know." Ade squeezed her hand. "But when Reet and I talked it over last night, we thought maybe there's a chance she could tell the story that we want told. Wouldn't it

175

be gratifying to wipe the smug smile off Grace's face, a chance to bring the golden girl down a peg or two?"

Wil nodded. Grace Green had been a little-known radio presenter when Kim met her. Then she'd gone on to become the most sought-after television interviewer and front person for important national events. Her rise to fame coincided with the deterioration of her relationship with Kim. In her recently released autobiography, she had made it look like she'd left Kim because of the writer's alcoholism. She had hinted at an abusive streak in the writer that came to the fore when she was drunk. None of that was remotely true. Grace had been obsessed with Kim to the end, and wouldn't leave her alone.

"Would it hurt to put Kim's side of the story out there?" Rita asked gently.

"I don't know." Wil felt the brightness of the morning take on a darker hue.

"Well, have a think about it. I will only arrange a meeting with her if you're agreeable to it." Ade stood and patted her shoulder. "I'll go down and see if any of the troops are up and about. I don't know when the card sharks stopped playing, but they were still at it when we went to bed."

†

It was all quiet downstairs when Ade arrived. Someone had turned the Christmas tree lights back on. She went into the study first and found it empty, the card table abandoned. After getting the fire going again, she walked over to the lounge to reset the fire there as well.

Only when she neared the kitchen were there any sounds of life. Candice was examining the contents of the fridge while Mags was busy with the coffee maker.

"Morning. Hope you both slept well." Ade greeted them cheerfully.

Mags looked round. "Yes, thanks. Like a log."

"No after-effects from the champagne."

"Not at all. And, thank you, by the way. The games were fun."

"Hey, we aim to please. Have you seen anyone else yet?"

"Signor Brunetti just left. He said he was going down to the stables. We thought we'd go down as well after we've eaten."

"Okay. Great. I'm sorry we can't offer the programme we normally do for Boxing Day."

"It's fine. We're used to snow. And I was kind of missing it this year."

Candice brought the package of bacon to the counter. "I'm doing bacon and eggs. Would you like some?"

"Thanks, but I've already eaten. Although the smell might tempt me."

Clare arrived in the kitchen, her hair wet from her swim. "Did someone mention bacon and eggs?"

"There's enough here for everyone." Candice looked up from the stove. "Why don't you see if you can round up JJ and Sal? We might as well eat together."

"Huddling together for warmth?" Ade joked.

"It's not so cold today." Mags was breaking eggs into a bowl. "I think it might start to thaw by lunchtime."

Ade smiled at them. It sometimes happened this way with guests, particularly at a holiday time. They formed a

177

bond. She guessed the previous day's swim had been the catalyst. Maybe they should incorporate it into their regular list of activities.

She left them to their breakfast plans and headed off to start her cleaning duties. The study would need hoovering as the dogs had spent a day and night in there. At least Guido and Felicity had refrained from smoking in the house. She suspected there would be a pile of cigarette butts by the front door, though.

By the time she had finished in the study and the lounge, she could hear the chatter coming from the dining room. Returning to the study to collect the card table, she was startled by a ringing sound. It took a moment to realise it was the phone. Picking up, she heard Mark's voice on the other end.

"Hello."

"Hello to you, too, and Merry Christmas, belatedly."

"You've all survived, then?"

"Yes, all good. And you?"

"No problem. We even had some customers yesterday. Anyway, just wanted to let you know, obviously the phone line is back up. So I contacted Tom Harris. As soon as he can get his tractor down his own track, he'll come and do yours. I told him it's a priority because of the baby being due any day."

"Thanks. What about the main road?"

"It's clear. Don't know where they dredged a snow plough from, but we heard it last night. That and the gritter. Just watched the weather news. We're not likely to get any more snow now."

"That's great."

"How's Gaby?"

"She's fine. We made her rest up yesterday though. Oh, and Wil finally got round to popping the question."

"Oh, excellent. Toby will be thrilled. He's got plans for the wedding cake."

Ade laughed. "Wil's idea for a quiet ceremony isn't going to happen, is it?"

"No. And best not tell her too much. Don't want to frighten her off the idea."

"Too right. Anyway, thanks for ringing. I'll let everyone know they're not going to be marooned here for much longer."

"Good. Hope to see you soon. Our beer sales are way down." He rang off before she could reply.

*Cheeky git.*

✝

"You know, I've never understood why the day after Christmas is called Boxing Day." Clare said, helping herself to another slice of bacon.

JJ looked at Sally for help. "I'm not sure. I thought maybe it was because it was a day when boxing matches were held. Nowadays, it's football."

"That's one idea. The more likely one," Sally offered, "is that it originated in Victorian times, when wealthy people would box up their leftovers to hand out to the poor of the parish. Now it's one of the biggest shopping days of the year. There will be news reports later about people being crushed in the Boxing Day sales."

"We have Boxing Day sales in Canada too," Candice said, through a mouthful of scrambled eggs.

"Those are a real con," Sally added. "They advertise a couple of big items at knockdown prices and the rest is just stuff they want to get rid of before new lines come in."

"Good thing we're snowed in. Not tempted to rush out and buy a big screen TV."

"We won't be snowed in for much longer."

They all turned to look at Ade.

"Several bits of good news. The main road through the village is clear. A local farmer will be coming along some time today with his tractor to clear our driveway. The Good Shepherd is open for business. Oh, and the phone lines are back up. I'll check on the Wi-Fi, but don't hold your breath. You may have to go to the pub if you want a decent signal strength."

JJ put her hand up. "Would it be all right for me to use the phone in the study again?"

Ade nodded. "Yes, that's fine. You might not want anything to eat for a while, but we will be providing the mulled wine and minced pies for elevenses, as advertised. Quiz sheets are available in the lounge for anyone who wants to take part. No cheating, if you do manage to get an Internet connection. Other than that, please relax, knowing that you're not stuck here for the rest of the week."

After she left, JJ made a move, getting up from the table. "Thanks for breakfast, Candice." She walked across the hall to the study, ready to put into action the plan she'd hatched during the night.

†

Candice looked around the table. "Anyone want more? There's a few rashers left."

180

"No, thanks. Sounds like there will be more eating opportunities later." Clare smiled at her. "Thanks for cooking, Candice. I'll do the washing up."

"Okay, that's great. We're going to go down to the stables."

"You won't be able to go riding in this. The snow's pretty deep in places."

"I know. We just want to see if we can help in any way. And just walking there and back will be good exercise. Do you have any plans, Sally?"

"I'll help Clare with the washing up."

When the other two had gone, Clare started to collect the plates, uncomfortably aware of Sally's eyes on her.

"I didn't expect you to rat me out. I thought we were friends."

Clare put the plates back on the table and sat down again. She met Sally's baleful stare. "I wouldn't say we're friends, exactly. Anyway, I thought Ade and Wil should know what you're up to."

"I only want to help."

"In what way? Dishing the dirt on Kim? Making money from making the people who loved her miserable?"

"That's not my intention. If anything, I could set the story straight. Grace Green shouldn't be allowed to have the last word."

Clare picked at the tablemat in front of her. "She wanted to interview me."

"Really? When was that?"

"A long time ago. I didn't speak to her directly, the contact was made via our respective agents."

"Was that before or after…you know…?"

"I slept with Kim." Clare finished the sentence for her and looked up. "After, obviously. She couldn't have cared less about talking to a relatively unknown Australian actress before." She paused. "I said no."

"Wow. I bet that would have been an interesting conversation."

Clare stood and picked up the plates again. "Nice try. You don't know when to give up, do you?" She walked through to the kitchen and started filling the sink with water. Looking out of the window, she could see snow starting to drip off the tree branches in the sunlight.

Maybe Sally was right. Telling their side of the story could help Kim's fans to understand the complexities of the writer's life. That she wasn't just a sad old alky who fell off her horse in one last drunken episode.

Sally came in and placed the coffee mugs on the counter next to the sink. Clare sighed and said, without turning around, "I'll talk to Ade. Maybe we can work something out."

"Thank you." The relief in the other woman's voice was evident.

"But don't get your hopes up. The main obstacle is Wil."

"Okay. I understand."

They worked together in companionable silence. Sally had just dried and put away the last of the cutlery when Rita and Gabriella arrived in the kitchen. They were both dressed for going outside. The younger woman had a large SLR camera slung around her neck, resting on her extended belly.

"We're going to get some photos before the snow melts away," Rita said.

"Ah," Clare had a flash of enlightenment. "The framed prints in the rooms, those are photographs you've taken," she said to Gaby.

"*Si.*"

"They're very beautiful."

Her smile was dazzling. "I live with beauty everywhere."

Rita took her arm. "Come on. We better do it before the sun moves around the house."

Clare hadn't realised she was holding her breath until they left the room. "Wow!" She breathed out slowly. "Wil Tyler is one lucky woman."

"She is." Sally leant back against the counter and Clare braced herself for another question, but when it came it wasn't what she'd expected. "So what was all that about with JJ last night?"

"I don't know what you mean."

"That snog under the mistletoe looked pretty hot."

"Oh that." Clare relaxed. "The poor woman's been dumped. She just needs reassurance that she's not a loser."

"Right. So did you throw in a comfort fuck as well?"

"Christ, Sally! Is that what you think of me? Anyway, she's not my type."

"What is your type?"

Clare smiled at her. "All right, I'll show you." She strode out of the kitchen sure that Sally would follow.

†

It was done now. No going back. JJ sank down into the sofa and watched the flames in the fireplace darting up the chimney. Johnny was a good lad. He'd promised not to tell her parents about Shelley's disappearance until she could do it herself when she got back home. As younger brothers went, he wasn't too much of a pain in the arse. And he was happy to help out by going around to her house and changing the locks.

Whatever Shelley's plans for the future were, they didn't include her and she wasn't going to make it easy. Shelley had walked out on their relationship without so much as a goodbye. It would have been a difficult conversation, but JJ would have liked to know what she'd done wrong. The anger was kicking in now. The cowardly bitch hadn't even had the guts to tell her what was going on. She'd just run away. But what was she running away from? During the long sleepless night, JJ couldn't recall any serious arguments over the last few months. Shelley had been a bit edgy the last few days but JJ put that down to the build-up to Christmas, sorting things out at work, their travel plans. JJ didn't know there was anything to be unhappy about. Everything had seemed normal.

Now, nothing would seem normal ever again.

†

Sally set off after the tall woman, running to keep up with her long-legged stride. She bumped into her when Clare stopped in the doorway to the dining room.

She opened her mouth, "What...?" Before she could finish the question, Clare pulled her close and kissed her, softly exploring her lips at first, and then demanding entry into her mouth with her tongue.

Sally lost all coherent thought as their bodies melded together and she enjoyed the sweetness of their mingled breaths.

"I'd say 'get a room,' but that's a bit unnecessary here." A voice interrupted their intimate moment just as it was getting interesting.

Clare relinquished her hold and gave Ade a piercing look. "Well, you shouldn't leave mistletoe hanging around in public places."

"Sorry to break this up, but actually I did want to speak to both of you."

Sally couldn't believe it. What did she want more? To go to bed with Clare, now? Or finally have a glimmer of hope that she would be getting the information she wanted for the book? She looked at Clare. Her face gave nothing away, but the light squeeze on her waist told her that there was more to come.

"Okay," she said calmly.

They moved into the dining room and Ade closed the door. Sitting down at the recently cleared breakfast table, Sally waited impatiently. She wanted to get back to that kiss and the promise it held of what it might lead to.

Ade looked at them and let out a deep breath before starting to speak. "I've talked to Wil and there is the possibility she may come round to the idea of this book, Sally. But you need to understand her reluctance. This is her home, her haven. She's worked hard to overcome many things from her early years, things that no one should have to experience, at any age. I'm sure you know the basics, so I'm not breaking any confidences here. Not only was her mother brutally murdered, but the press reports made it sound like she deserved it, branding her a whore and a thief. Wil went into foster care and suffered abuse from her supposed caretakers. Kim was the only stable point in her life at the time. She gradually came to trust Rita and myself as well. We became her family. Then that, too, was broken when Kim died. Thankfully, she'd met Gaby at that point, because without her unfailing love and support, I doubt even we would have been able to get her through those dark days."

Sally met her intense gaze unflinchingly. "I understand. And I'm sorry I've gone about this in such a cack-handed manner. My aim for this book is to give people a better view of Kim as a person. She was obviously well loved by all of you." She avoided looking at Clare as she spoke. "I want to be able to show that side of her, a complete person, not just written off as an alcoholic. I know you want to protect her memory and I totally get that. But I also think you don't want Grace Green's air-brushed version of events to be the last word on Kim's life."

"No, we don't." Wil walked into the room from the door that led to the kitchen.

From the looks on Ade's and Clare's faces, they hadn't noticed her presence before.

Wil sat down at the head of the table and looked at each of them in turn. Sally wondered how much she had heard.

"Happiness. They say you don't recognise it until it's taken away. I've had a lot of things taken away from me, but I've also been given a lot. I think, on balance, I've come out on top. Sorry, if that doesn't make much sense. Everything's changing. Once the baby is born, our lives won't be the same. I've had nine months to prepare for that. It's taken me over a year to ask Gaby to marry me. I don't know why I waited so long. And now, maybe, I can lay some ghosts to rest as well. If it truly is your aim, Sally, to present Kim's life in a positive light, then I'm happy for you to go ahead. Clare, I know you have reservations about taking part in this new *Shay Finch* series, but it will happen with or without you. So, if you want to do it, that's fine with me. The dragons of change, once seen, there's no going back." She stood and left as abruptly as she had entered.

Sally looked from Clare to Ade and back again. "The dragons of change?"

"It's an ancient myth," Clare said. "If you look on the dragons of change, things will happen in your life."

"Well, where did that come from? I mean, I'm extremely grateful that she's given me a green light for the book, but..."

"I don't know where it came from either," Ade said. "Wil's a deep one. You never really know what's going on in her head. Anyway, I'll leave you to it. I believe you have your own unfinished business. I'll catch up with you later."

Sally looked at Clare after she'd gone. "Do we have unfinished business?"

"We sure do. Your room or mine?"

†

Candice linked her arms through her partner's as they trudged back up to the house on the now well-beaten path through the snow. By the time they had reached the stables after their leisurely breakfast, the horses had all been fed and watered. Rose had finished the mucking out, so she and Mags helped Guido clear a section of the yard to make it possible to exercise the animals later. The dogs had already tired themselves out after an initial bout of frantic energy from having spent the day before indoors.

Felicity invited Candice and Mags into the Lodge for a well-earned cup of coffee, and they had spent an enjoyable half hour talking with the older people who had questions for them about Canada. Rose said she had relatives who lived in a place called Livelong, Saskatchewan, and did they know them. Candice had to admit she'd never been to Saskatchewan. Whenever they visited Marguerite's family, they flew to Montreal, passing over the Prairie Provinces and northern Ontario.

As they neared the house, Mags suggested they take a look at their car. "If this stuff starts to melt, it'll be heavy to shift. We should probably scrape off what we can now."

"Well, let's hope this farmer guy doesn't cover it up again when he clears the drive."

The snow lay thickly by the house where no one had been, and the drift came up over the edges of their borrowed boots as they made their own track around to the front.

Mags ducked just in time as a snowball flew past her head. She looked up to see a shocked look on Wil's face.

"Sorry, it was meant for her." Wil pointed to Ade who was standing a few feet away, holding a missile of her own and grinning.

"Good."

Candice saw that Mags had picked up a handful of snow when she ducked and was fashioning it into a ball behind her back. She moved out of the way and Mags threw a perfect curve ball that caught the unsuspecting Ade square in the chest.

The ensuing snowball fight was threatening to get serious when Rita poked her head out of the door, told them recess was over, and they should come in to warm up with mulled wine and mince pies.

Candice noticed that both cars had been cleared of snow along with a wide area around them. She thanked Wil as they removed their outdoor gear in the hall.

"No problem. We'll put some sand down after Tom's been and make sure we can move them."

Mags grabbed her before they went into the lounge and whispered in her ear. "Thank you. This has been one of the best Christmases ever."

Candice agreed wholeheartedly and relaxed against her as they kissed.

"Hey, this is a mistletoe-free zone." Ade laughed, passing them with a tray of mugs.

They pulled apart but Candice could see the sparkle in her lover's eyes. She was glad they had made this trip, making a break from their usual routine of visiting their families at Christmas. The last few days had seen the return of the Mags she had hoped would eventually come back to her.

†

Clare looked down at the blonde head nestled against her breasts and played with the soft strands of hair. The delightful curves of the other woman's body hadn't escaped her notice when they were cavorting in the pool the night before. Thoughts of it had kept her awake for some time.

Her tummy rumbled, and Sally stirred.

"Sounds like I could eat some food again, although it feels like that's all we've done for three days."

Sally sat up and her eyes travelled down the length of Clare's body. Finally, she spoke, "So, is this the beginning of something, or the end?"

"What do you mean?"

Trailing her fingers across Clare's abdomen before resting her hand on the tangle of now wet curls, Sally said, "I guess I'm wondering if you'll be sticking around. Now that you have Wil's blessing to take the Shay Finch role."

"I might be. Staying in London is expensive though."

"I can offer you lodging. Although the standard isn't up to the Ritz or whatever fancy hotels you are used to."

"And what would you expect in payment?"

"This." Sally's hand strayed down between her legs.

Clare moaned and moved her hips to meet the searching fingers.

"Can I take that as an acceptance?" Sally's fingers moved further in and she slowly started a rocking motion.

"I'm coming."

"I know you are," Sally closed in on her mouth and sealed the deal with a penetrating kiss.

†

Ade did a head count. Candice and Mags had followed her into the house. JJ was in the lounge reading a book. Sally and Clare had come into the room shortly after and it didn't require any brainpower to know what they had been doing. They were both wearing self-satisfied smiles, and luckily wearing clothes.

Wil had checked briefly on the fire and said she was going into the study. She thought Gaby would be in there after her outdoor photo session.

190

Rita and Teresa were in the kitchen preparing yet more food for lunch and starting on the dinner prep. The other three were staying down at the stables and would eat at the Lodge.

"What are you reading"? Mags asked JJ as she sat down opposite.

JJ held up the cover so Mags could see it.

"Oh, which one is that?"

"Number Four."

"That was my favourite, of the films. I haven't read any of the books."

"It's good."

Sally joined JJ on her sofa and said, "Four and seven are the best."

Ade looked up as Clare approached her. "Are you serving, or do we help ourselves?"

"I'll do the drink, you can help yourself to mince pies. Two mulled wines?"

"Yes, thanks."

"So, fast work?" Ade nodded in Sally's direction.

"Christmas bonus. I could get to like your Boxing Day customs."

"I don't think shagging in the morning is necessarily a standard ritual."

"It wasn't just a shag."

"Ooh, serious stuff."

"Maybe. I don't know. Time will tell."

"You'll be staying around, then?"

"Looks like it." Clare took the mugs from her. "I'll come back for the pies."

Ade watched her go over to Sally, hand her the drink and perch on the arm of the sofa, draping her other arm casually around the other woman's shoulders. Sally's smile, as she looked up at her, had an intensity to it Ade hadn't seen from her before.

*Love or lust?* As Clare had said, time would tell.

†

Gaby wasn't in the study, so Wil used the internal line on the phone to call upstairs to their room. No answer. She tried the kitchen extension and Rita answered.

"Yes, she's here. But don't worry, we're making her sit and supervise."

Wil smiled to herself. Any prolonged inactivity drove Gaby crazy. Just as she put the receiver down, the phone rang. She picked up, thinking it would probably be Mark.

"Wilma."

She recognised the voice immediately, although it wasn't one she had heard in many years. "Thelma."

"I tried to ring yesterday, but it sounded like your line was dead."

"Yes, it was down all day. What can I do for you?" Wil struggled to keep her tone neutral.

"I wanted to get in touch with one of your guests, Sally Hunter. I've left messages on her mobile, but she's not responded."

"Our Wi-Fi has taken a holiday as well. She won't have been able to get a signal." After a pause, Wil added, more forcefully, "Don't you think you should have told me about the Shay Finch stuff you found?"

"Ah, well, it all happened so quickly. And it's out of my hands now."

"I trusted you."

"Look, Kim was my friend, too. I wouldn't do anything I thought would harm her."

"Just make money out of her. You did well out of Amy, now you can capitalise on Shay as well. You do know Clare Finlayson is here, too?"

"No, I didn't know that, although I knew the producer was keen to talk to her. Well, well, that is interesting." Thelma sounded like Miss Marple, but Wil wasn't falling for the kindly old lady act. Not again.

"I'll ask Sally to call you," she said firmly and put the phone down.

Thelma Barton. A voice from the past and a reminder of a conversation from long ago when the woman turned up at the house unexpectedly. At a time when Wil was still coming to terms with Kim's sudden death.

…"So, what do you want to talk about?"

"Well, as you probably know, I was Kim's editor at Red Knight. We've recently been approached by the film company in Australia who made the first six Amy Ransom films. They want to do the seventh. As Kim's executor, your permission is needed."

"Don't they already have the rights to it?"

"No. Kim was very cautious about signing the whole series away. She would only agree to one book at a time. She may have been a piss-head, but she was very astute about business matters."

Wil couldn't look at the woman. If she hadn't been sitting down with a table between them she would have lashed out.

"Look, I can leave it with you to mull over. But they want an answer soon. The ideal time to start filming in Oz is September."

Wil looked at her then, keeping her voice level. "Maybe I should come up to London. I need to see my solicitor anyway. How about Monday?"

Thelma nodded. "Fine. It would be good if you spoke to our MD, Richard Everett, as well. He's done most of the negotiating with the Aussies." She took a deep breath before continuing. "Do you know if Kim left any unfinished works? We think she was working on Amy number ten before she died."

Wil's head came up from examining the burn mark on the table that had suddenly acquired a new level of fascination. "No. I haven't looked." She had, with Ade's help, boxed up Kim's stuff. Her clothes had mostly been binned; there were a few men's suits that were in good enough condition to give to charity shops. She only kept Kim's leather jacket and the Australian bush hat she had treasured. Kim's computer, laptop, disks, and paper files were stored in her bedroom, but Wil hadn't been able to face going through any of it.

Thelma persisted. "It might be worth a look," she continued, seemingly unaware of the pain she was causing. "We're planning to reissue the Amy Ransom series next spring. It would be great to have something new to tie in with it."

Wil didn't answer. She really wanted this woman to go away.

"Look, I know this may not be the best time to ask, but why did you stop writing?"

Wil looked at her blankly.

"The story you sent in for the anthology. It was you, wasn't it...Wanda Taylor? I recognised Kim's handwriting on the envelope. For a long time I thought it was her story, although clearly not her style. She always denied it. It makes sense now, meeting you. You must have been, what, fourteen?"

"Yeah." It seemed a lifetime ago. "Shit happened."

"Well, if you ever write anything else, I'd be happy to see it. You showed definite promise."

"Thanks."

Thelma stood. "Just let me know what time you're arriving on Monday." She fished a card out of her pocket and put it on the table. "Thanks for the coffee."

Wil continued staring into space long after the door closed behind her...

The story was one she had written when she was at school before the move to Winterbourne, a story of unrequited love, and her first girl crush. That was how she had first met Kim. They hadn't been in the village long. Her mother had set herself up as a hairdresser in the cottage they rented, and Wil started taking riding lessons at the stables. Of course, like everyone in the village, they were curious about the new owner of Winterbourne House. A well-known author in their midst was quite a novelty, a lesbian writer bordered on the most exciting bit of news the village had known in several centuries.

Wil endured three lessons, bumping around on a patient horse like a sack of potatoes, before finally plucking up the courage to talk to the writer.

...Another bright summer's day. Wil walked up the long drive, still in her riding gear, wondering what she would say if she did actually come face to face with Kim Russell. The house looked deserted when she reached it. She walked around to the back and there she was, sitting at a table, notepad in front of her with a glass containing an amber liquid within reach. Tales of her drinking habits were already a legend as her housekeeper was the local gossip.

Kim looked up and seemed amused to see her.

"Hello," she said. "Lost your way? The stables are at the other end of the drive."

"No. I've had my lesson. I was looking for you." She was pleased to get the words out without stammering although she was sure she was red in the face.

"Oh. Why would you be looking for me?"

"I wanted to meet you."

"Why?"

"I want to be a writer."...

And that was the start. Kim hadn't laughed at her. Wil had never shown her writing to anyone, least of all her mother. But somehow she immediately felt a connection with Kim. Her initial embarrassment melted away as they talked that first afternoon. A week later when she returned, Kim had not only read her story, but made some notes on it and told her it had merit. She'd written Thelma Barton's name and the Red Knight publisher's address on a large brown envelope and told her to send it. Thelma was looking for submissions from new writers for an anthology.

Wil didn't hear anything from the publisher and her interest in writing as a career stalled. She was only thankful that her passion for languages, through high school and university, led her to Rome and meeting Gabriella. She didn't want to contemplate what her life would have been like without Gaby.

But the biggest "if only" from that time was what still gave her chills in the middle of the night. If she hadn't gone to see Kim with her putative writing, Kim wouldn't have met her mother. And if they hadn't met, then neither Kim nor her mother would be dead. And she wouldn't be living here. But if she followed those "ifs" through, then she wouldn't have met Gaby either.

She stared at the phone, her thoughts jumbling around in her head. Today it seemed everyone was conspiring to remind her of the friend she had lost. She wished Kim could have met Gaby. It was what the writer had wanted for Wil, to see her settled. Engaged, soon to be married, having a baby, Kim wouldn't have envisaged any of this, but it's what she would have loved to see.

Wil shook her head. She had a message to deliver.

†

Sally reviewed her conversation with the old woman. Thelma had said that Wil had been short with her on the phone, bordering on hostility.

"She's got a lot on her mind," Sally had responded, wondering at her own protective feelings towards Wil.

After letting Thelma know that she was making some progress with the plans for the book, she told her she would probably stay on for a few more days. If she couldn't stay at the house, there was a B&B in the village.

197

"I need to take it slow, Thel. No point in frightening the horses. I think they'll talk to me. It's just going to have to be in their own time."

"Well don't take too long about it. I'm not getting any younger."

Sally promised to keep her informed of any further developments before ending the call. She sat down on one of the sofas and stared at the fireplace. Someone, Gabriella probably, had decorated the mantelpiece with sprigs of holly.

There was so much to this story, and now that she had started, she was determined to persevere. The story of how Kim Russell, who had started out as a homeless teenager, ended up in a mansion house—with a hundred-and-fifty acres of prime real estate in the middle of Sussex—and then passed it on to someone else who had started out with nothing. Less than nothing, because Wil had been orphaned as well.

Sally opened her notebook and looked at the timeline and outline she'd been working on for the biography. The early years would be a very short section. From what she had gleaned from reading archived newspaper articles, the writer had grown up in a middle-class family in a leafy London suburb, and left home after her parents found her in bed with the local vicar's daughter. There was likely more to that story, since once she had left, she had no further contact with her family. But Sally wasn't sure how she could find out unless Kim had confided in Ade.

As if summoned by her thoughts, the door opened and Ade came in. "Ah, there you are. Lunch will be ready in a few minutes."

"Right. Sorry, I guess I shouldn't still be in here, but I just wanted to make a few notes." Sally closed her notebook and stood, trying not to feel intimidated by the taller woman's presence. "Not much is known about Kim's childhood, is it?"

Ade grimaced and Sally wondered if she'd overstepped the mark, again. But the answer, when it came, was so simple she could have kicked herself for not thinking of it herself.

"AR1, it's all in there. And in some of the other books, explaining why Amy reacts to certain situations the way she does."

"Oh, of course. Thanks." Sally followed Ade out into the hall.

Ade stopped before the door to the dining room. Sally noticed, inconsequentially, that the mistletoe was no longer there. "We'll meet with you after lunch. Unless you and Clare have other plans." This time, Sally did get a genuine smile.

"Um, no. I mean, yes, that would be great."

"Okay, see you later." Ade strode off towards the kitchen and Sally opened the door to the dining room.

†

The lunch provided was simple fare. Another Boxing Day custom Clare gathered, making use of the leftovers from the day before. Nicely presented leftovers, though, and with a selection of fresh fruit. She peeled a tangerine and listened to the conversation across the table. Candice, who was talking about their plans for the rest of their trip before they returned to Canada, suddenly turned to JJ.

"We can give you a ride, if you want. We're heading up your way next."

JJ looked surprised. "What, all the way to Manchester?"

"Yes, we'll be going on to Liverpool. That's sort of on the way, isn't it?"

"Well, yeah, that would be great. And, if you want to stop over, I can offer you a bed for the night."

Clare smiled at the three of them. They seemed to have bonded. It would be good for JJ not to have to travel back alone, and to an empty house. She was aware of Sally, sitting next to her, subdued after her mystery phone call.

"What are your plans, Sally?" Candice asked, as if reading Clare's mind.

"Thought I'd stick around for a few days. I'll book into the Bed and Breakfast place. It's near the pub, which I understand does good food as well."

"I wouldn't have thought you'd want to eat again after what we've had here."

"Once the snow's cleared, I'll be able to get some walks in. Work up an appetite."

"Clare?"

"Candice." Clare was used to the Canadian's straightforward manner now.

"What about you? Are you sticking around?"

"In the country, yes. I have some business to attend to in London." Clare avoided looking at Sally. She wasn't sure what she wanted. They had another night together here, a chance to further explore what they had started. No need to rush into anything.

# Chapter Seven

## The Thaw

Guido followed in Felicity's footsteps as he led another horse around the yard. She was leading Paddy, Wil's mare. He had the more sedate Shadow, who seemed content to walk slowly, sniffing the fresh clean air.

Felicity had been quiet throughout their lunch together, leaving the conversation to him and Rose. He thought it was the call from Rita that had unsettled her. He'd only caught a few words that made sense to him. One of the guests was writing a book, a biography of Kim Russell.

During their recent tack room chats, Felicity had told him quite a bit about the writer. How she hadn't expected to like Kim when she arrived to take over the house following the death of her uncle, Philip Russell. He had been a heavy drinker and that gene was passed on to his niece. At first, Felicity had tried to maintain her distance, keeping an employee/employer relationship. But the more she saw of Kim, the more she realised there was someone vulnerable under the tough exterior Kim projected. As time went on, Felicity found herself wanting to protect her, save her from hurt.

"She should never have taken up with that hairdresser woman. I knew she'd be trouble," Felicity had confided to Guido only the other day. "But then Wil wouldn't be here."

That she had a soft spot for Wil was no secret. Feeling she had failed with Kim, keeping Wil safe was her priority. An outsider wouldn't have known it from the way they spoke to each other. Wil pretended she didn't need Felicity's care and the older woman feigned indifference. But the love between them was evident in their actions.

"Why?" Guido had asked. "What was she like?" He genuinely wanted to know more about Wil's mother. When he'd asked Gaby, she said Wil never talked about her.

"She was a taker. But Kim was blind to that. Obsessed. Possessed more like. That woman was poison. Ginny would have drained Kim's lifeblood, like a vampire."

Ginny. It was the first time he'd heard the name. When he talked to his wife later she told him it was a shortened version of Virginia.

Once started on the subject of the soul-destroying Ginny, Felicity couldn't stop. "She did almost kill Kim."

Guido thought the story sounded like something out of one of the crime novels Teresa was so fond of reading. At the time Kim met the life-sucking hairdresser, she was dividing her time between Winterbourne and the house she owned in London. This continued when they started living together. Wil had arrived at the London house for the holidays—she was now a weekly boarder at a school in Brighton—to find it empty. Not just empty, the living room was trashed—pictures off the walls, broken glass everywhere, ripped and broken furniture. Frightened out of her wits, she ran all the way to Ade's, which was only a few streets away. Ade phoned the police and not getting any joy there, rang around the hospitals. And that's when they found out Kim had been in a car accident.

Felicity paused long enough to light another cigarette before continuing with the tale. "She was a mess. The doctors thought she'd crashed the car because she was drunk. But Kim was a good driver even when over the limit. No, she wanted to die. Ade got the truth out of her eventually. The final fight with Ginny. Kim could have defended herself, but she didn't. I'd seen it often enough. Whenever Ginny lost her temper, Kim would walk away. She was just getting over the worst of her injuries when the police turned up at her door to tell her they'd found Ginny. You see, Kim had reported her missing. She still wanted her back."

This part of the story confused Guido. Why would she want her back? The woman sounded like a disaster-magnet.

"It took Kim a long time to recover from the news of what had happened to Ginny. She was found in a ditch near Nottingham. Brutally murdered and raped. I may not have liked the woman, but I wouldn't have wished that on her. I just wanted her to leave Kim alone. Then Kim fell for that bitch, Grace. But that's another story altogether."

He knew all about Grace. Gaby had explained to him why the television presenter's recent autobiography had so upset Wil and Ade.

"You mustn't tell Wil I've told you this." Felicity insisted. "She won't talk about it but I know it worries her. She's afraid she'll be a bad parent. That Ginny's genes will take over. My theory is that Ginny wasn't even her mother. I think she picked her up somewhere so she could get single mother benefits. The only trait Wil has of hers is the red hair.

No sign whatsoever of the raging temper or controlling nature."

Guido could agree. He only had to see Wil with Gaby to know true love when he saw it. His friends back home couldn't understand how he could so happily accept his daughter's lifestyle. Bad enough being a lesbian, but moving to England as well, that was almost worse in their eyes. But from the first moment he'd seen the two of them together, he knew Wil and Gaby were meant for each other. They had been kids when they met, but they had grown into fine young women and he was proud of both of them.

†

Ade sat next to Wil and watched Sally find her place in her notebook. Clare had joined them and was sitting on the hearth.

"Okay." Sally looked up from her notes. "This is my initial idea for structuring the book. A fairly short chapter on her early years, as I guess there's not much to tell…"

"I was born," muttered Clare.

Ade knew that was a line from the first paragraph of *David Copperfield* by Charles Dickens. She wasn't sure how she knew that. Must have paid some attention during English classes at school.

Sally continued. "Following that, a chapter on her career as a journalist before she started writing the Amy Ransom novels. That's where you come in, Ade, as I guess you knew her best at that time. I know the next bit is painful for you guys, but I will have to include a section on your mother, Wil. I was planning to talk to Felicity…"

"Good luck with that," Wil said, concentrating her gaze on the carpet between her feet.

"The next part would be about her relationship with Grace. I guess you could both help to fill in the gaps there. Then, Clare, if you wouldn't mind, something about when you met and how she felt about the film versions of her books." Sally looked over at the actress who seemed to be finding something fascinating in the brickwork of the fireplace.

"The last chapter will be the hardest to write. The obituaries I've found online don't go into much detail. I guess Felicity was here when she died. The coroner's verdict was accidental death, but there was some suggestion it may have been suicide. But that was never proven."

Ade couldn't look at Wil. They had talked about this many times. There was a letter, which only they knew about. It had been handwritten so they were certain there was no digital version that could come to light.

"Well, that all sounds fine." Wil stood and ignored Ade's attempt to pull her back down, moving quickly out of reach. "I think I hear Tom's tractor. He must be getting close to the house. Catch up with you later."

When the door closed behind her, Ade shrugged and said, "I don't mind talking about Grace. It's harder for Wil, and she was only a kid when the relationship first started, so her take on things will be different to mine."

"So, what was it like? How did they meet? It must have been a bit of culture clash. Cut glass meets rough diamond."

Ade noticed that Clare's gaze had returned to the room. She was, no doubt, also interested in how Kim had become involved with someone like Grace Green, an aristocrat's daughter.

"I guess I better start at the beginning," Ade said, settling back in her seat.

…Kim was interviewed for radio by Grace Green and didn't have a clue who she was. Kim rarely listened to cultural programmes. But Ade knew and when talking to Kim after she returned to her secluded life at Winterbourne, she encouraged Kim to take up the invitation that had come through the post.

Ade had called Kim to confirm arrangements for a visit to introduce her to the new woman in her life. The conversation was one she remembered well.

"Rita would like to come. How about this weekend?"

"Yeah okay, if you're sure."

"You don't sound so enthusiastic."

"It's just that I've been invited to a, well, to a horse thing. I won't be around Saturday afternoon. I'll cancel though, if you're definitely coming."

"No, no. You go. I'm sure we can amuse ourselves for a few hours."

"Well, as long as you don't mind..."

"Who's the invite from?"

"I'll ignore the bad grammar. It's from Sir Antony Coombes, a neighbour apparently."

"Oh, that's interesting."

"You've heard of him?"

"I know of him."

"He knew my uncle."

"Yes, that is interesting. You should definitely go."

"Ade, are you pulling my leg?"

"No, I wouldn't dream of it. See you Friday, about nine."

Ade had an inkling that the invitation had been issued at the request of Sir Antony's daughter, a connection that Kim wouldn't have been aware of. And Ade had been proved right. What she hadn't expected was that Miss Green would turn out to be such a fast worker. Something that became apparent later was how the quiet persona hid a steely determination. When she wanted something, Grace was used to getting it. And she wanted Kim.

That weekend had been interesting in more ways than one. Rita had commented drily, on their way back to London, that it was better than watching back-to-back episodes of Coronation Street. Who knew that country living was so full of drama.

On Sunday morning, Ade and Rita were suffering from a bit of a hangover. They had spent too much time at The Good Shepherd waiting for Kim to return from the horse races. Then Wil turned up. She'd run away from the people who had taken her in after her mother's death. Coping with a distraught fourteen-year-old who had somehow managed to travel two-hundred miles across the country, without any money, was more than enough for one morning. Ade offered to go and wake Kim, but Felicity, who always knew more than she let on, said she would go.

Kim eventually made it to the kitchen and her appearance didn't take much interpreting as to what activity she had been engaged in during the night. Ade pressed a cup of strong coffee into her hand before suggesting she take Wil outside to talk to her.

When the youngster returned to the kitchen, she was smiling.

"Everything okay, sweetheart?" Rita had asked gently.

"She said she would sort it. Who's that woman?"

"What woman?" Ade asked, although she now thought she could guess.

And that was the start. Grace Green grabbed hold of Kim and was reluctant to let go, even when it was obvious to everyone around them that it wasn't working out. Grace couldn't leave Kim alone, and in the early days of their relationship, it was probably what the writer needed with all the trauma she'd experienced with Ginny. But after a while Kim started to feel trapped and her alcohol intake increased. Grace wasn't used to not having control but she couldn't stop Kim's drinking habits. She couldn't understand why loving Kim wasn't enough to make her change…

Ade came back to the present aware of the others in the room. Sally was hunched over her notebook and recorder making notes.

Clare stood abruptly. "I should have come back with her. She'd still be alive now if I had." Her eyes brimming with tears, she strode from the room.

Sally gazed after her, a look of hurt on her face.

"Hey, what did you expect? The questions you're asking are going to bring up a lot of memories. If you're interested in a relationship with Clare, it's something you'll have to deal with."

"Great. How do I compete with a dead woman?"

"I don't know. But to make a start, you might want to go after Clare now. Talk to her."

Sally closed her notebook and hurried out.

Ade sat back and wondered if she'd missed her calling. Relationship counselling, what a thought!

†

Wil waved to Tom and waited for him to switch off the tractor before approaching. He clambered down and greeted her with a bear hug.

"Thanks for doing this."

"Well, when Mark told me the bairn's due any second, Emma told me to get this lot cleared pronto. She has a few other patients to check on today but she said to tell you she'll be by later this afternoon."

"Emma's a gem," Wil made a mental note to thank the farmer's wife for her thoughtfulness. "Do you have time to come in for a hot drink? And a mince pie, or three?"

Tom laughed. "For one of Gabriella's pies, I'll clear the rest of your land."

"That's not necessary. Come on in. Coffee or mulled wine?"

†

The knock on the bedroom door startled Clare out of her reverie. She didn't want to talk to anyone, but she knew who it would be and called out, "Come in."

Sally stood in the doorway, looking uncertain about whether or not she was welcome. Clare gave her a wan smile and gestured for her to join her on the two-seater couch by the window. Neither of them spoke as they both stared out at the view. The snow was melting rapidly off the tree branches and the snow horse was now headless.

209

"The other day, in the clearing. You were thinking about her then, weren't you?" Sally hesitantly placed a hand on her thigh.

Clare looked down at the hand, smaller and paler than the one she placed on top of it. "Yes. I wasn't sure coming here was such a good idea. Some memories are probably best left in the past."

"But eventually you have to face them. Maybe that's why you wanted to be here." Sally's tone was softer than usual.

"Twenty years is a long time to hang on to something so intangible. Am I still so naive as to think I could have saved her?" Clare took a deep breath. "I was twenty-five when I met her. Getting the Shay Finch part in the Amy Ransom film was my first major role, a big step up from playing bit parts. Maybe it had gone to my head. I hadn't even met any real lesbians at that point. My unrequited crushes were all on women I wouldn't have dared to approach. Teachers, actresses I'd only seen on screen. Apart from a few fumblings with school chums who just wanted to experiment, practice kissing, I had never been with a woman. Kim was my first."

"That explains a lot. Although it surprises me. I wouldn't have thought you'd have any trouble attracting women."

"Attracting them, yes. Knowing what to do with them, that was another matter. Believe it or not, I was painfully shy in those days."

Sally increased the pressure on her thigh. "I guess it makes sense. The connection you still feel. I don't think you ever forget your first love."

"So, why didn't I follow my heart?" Clare shook her head. "I do know the answer to that. For Kim, it was a holiday romance. Once the filming finished, she would be returning home, back to her real life. I knew she had a partner. But I didn't know they were having problems, she never talked about Grace. She did talk about Wil though. And she talked a lot about Wil's mother. I was jealous of Ginny for a time until Kim told me she'd died."

"I'm sorry."

Clare looked at her, surprised to see tears coursing down her face. "What are you sorry about?"

"Bringing it all up. All these sad memories for you, for Wil and Ade. Maybe writing this book is a stupid idea."

"No." Clare put her arm around Sally's shoulders and held her. "I think you should write it. There are good memories too. Talking about it can only help us all put our feelings in perspective."

†

After lunch, even though she hadn't eaten much, JJ felt she needed a walk. The sun was helping to melt the snow rapidly. Already there were clear patches of grass showing through where tracks had been made with the snowshoes.

It seemed a shame that the snow horse, created with so much effort only the day before, was now degrading into a heap of misshapen lumps. She breathed in the fresh air, realising that apart from the dash to the pool and back the night before she hadn't been outside for two days. Not since she and Shelley had walked down to the pub on Christmas Eve. *Was that really only two days ago?* She shook her head, she wasn't going to spoil the day by giving in to melancholy thoughts. Fresh air and exercise were what she needed after a restless night. With any luck she could tire herself out enough that falling asleep would come easily when she went to bed later.

The track ended at the stable door and JJ decided to take a look at the horses inside. Sounds of the large animals shuffling about in their stalls greeted her ears, while her nose was assaulted by a strong smell she was unfamiliar with. When her eyes adjusted to the gloom, she could see horses' heads hanging over their half doors. Their eyes followed her as she walked cautiously down the middle of the walkway. A stall door at the end was open, and when she looked in, she saw someone brushing the horse's back with long flowing strokes, humming to herself.

"Um, hi," she said, unsure whether or not she should be interrupting what looked like a pleasurable ritual for both horse and human.

The person looked round and JJ realised it was Rose. She'd been seated opposite her during the Christmas lunch. They hadn't exchanged any words, but the horsewoman had chatted easily with the others at their end of the table, Rita and the Italian couple, Gabriella's parents.

"Hello." Rose gave her a pleasant smile and gestured for her to come in. "You can pet him, he doesn't bite."

The horse had turned its head, possibly to see why Rose had stopped mid-brush.

"His name's Shadow." She dug her free hand into her jacket pocket and produced a carrot. "Here, give him this and you'll have a friend for life."

JJ took the carrot from her and regarded the horse's head cautiously. "I've never done this before."

"It's okay. Just hold it flat on the palm of your hand. Keep your fingers together."

Following these instructions, JJ held her hand out towards the horse's head. He sniffed, rather delicately, she thought, before picking up the carrot and crunching it between his large teeth.

"Wow. That's amazing. Such soft lips." JJ stroked the long nose.

Rose resumed her brushing.

"Looks like he's enjoying that."

"Yes. They all do. They like the attention."

"A bit like humans."

"Of course."

"Can I do anything to help?"

Rose looked at her again. "You're a guest. We don't usually put you to work."

"I would like to do something. Take my mind off things."

"Okay. Well, if I show you what to do, you can carry on with Shadow here. Now that he knows you. And I'll just be in the next stall with Paddy."

By the time she set off back to the house a few hours later, JJ felt like an accomplished horsewoman. She had groomed two more horses. Then Rose led Shadow outside and showed her how to put on the bridle and saddle. With Rose's gentle persuasion she had been encouraged to climb onto his back, not very expertly, needing a final push to get up. Once seated, with the stirrups adjusted to the right length, Rose led them both around the yard.

"You're a natural," Rose had said after she clambered off awkwardly. "We could have you hitting the trails around here in no time."

JJ thought that if she hadn't been heading home the next day, she would have liked to take her up on that offer. Maybe she could try horse riding as a hobby. Finding stables near where she lived shouldn't be difficult. Shelley had never wanted to do anything that involved exercise. JJ's job as a decorator was active enough for her to keep fit, but doing something for enjoyment was an idea she hadn't considered before. Trading in her ex-lover for a horse—JJ was smiling broadly as she entered the house.

†

Candice let her body float lazily, resting her head and arms on the edge of the pool, while Mags swam energetically up and down doing a proper swimmer's crawl. Candice sometimes managed a few laps with a languid breaststroke. She preferred to keep her head above water at all times.

When Mags joined her, flushed and breathless from her exertions, she gave her a dazzling smile shaking wet hair from her face. "I've been thinking…"

"You need to stop that. We're on holiday, my love," Candice grinned back at her.

"No, really. When we get back home, I'm going to apply to join the RCMP."

"Seriously?" Candice looked into her eyes. "You've had one ride on a horse and you want to be a Mountie?"

"No, silly. That would involve six months at their training camp in Saskatchewan, and then getting posted to anywhere in Canada. I meant as a civilian. There are bound to be some openings in the Vancouver area, possibly in their marine services."

"Looks like you have given this some serious thought."

"Well, I need to do something positive." Mags draped a wet arm across her shoulders. "I know the nightmares won't go away completely. I know it's been hard for you and you've been so patient."

"It's no hardship. I love you, sweetheart. However long it takes, I'm here for you."

Mags gave her a tremulous smile before kissing her soundly on the lips. When she pulled away, her voice was husky as she said; "I think we should go back to our room so I can show you how much I appreciate your love."

Candice thought she probably set a world record for getting out of the pool, drying off, dressing, and running back to the house.

†

Wil stayed in the kitchen after Tom left, alone with her thoughts for the first time that day. Her earlier worries of how Sally would treat Kim in her biography were starting to fade. Maybe it was time to let go, to stop replaying the past. Felicity had once asked her why she wanted to stay at Winterbourne if it reminded her so much of Kim. She didn't have an answer for her then, but she did now.

The meeting with the solicitor all those years ago was one of those scenes that often came back to her in the darkest hours of the night.

...She had still been reeling from the shock of learning about Kim's sudden death. Wil was worn down from lack of sleep after the frantic drive through France to make it back to London in time for the funeral service. The funeral had taken place only the day before, and Wil wasn't sure she could go through with this meeting without breaking down. Kim's instructions for the service had been followed to the letter; Ade had even managed to find a female non-denominational minister to conduct it. Grace had been present but she and Wil hadn't made eye contact and Wil rushed off afterwards without speaking to anyone.

The solicitor placed his hands on the document in front of him. "The first time I met Kim, I had to talk to her about her uncle's death. It came as a terrible shock to her, as I'm sure this has to you. Have you been told how she died?"

Will nodded again, this time managing to find her voice. "Ade said she had a riding accident."

"Yes, well that's the official version. What you may not know, what she didn't let anyone know, is that she was very ill. It was her liver, of course. And cirrhosis is not a pleasant way to die."

"You think she killed herself?"

"It can't be proven conclusively, and the coroner returned a verdict of accidental death, but the conversation I've had subsequently with Mrs Evans makes me think that might not be the case. She rode out on one of the partly trained stallions, not her usual mount, I understand. It wouldn't have taken much to spook him. She was taking a risk though. If the fall hadn't killed her, she could have ended up severely disabled."

Wil swallowed hard. She was struggling to hold back the tears.

"I know," the solicitor continued in a sympathetic tone. "She was only forty-four, a good ten years younger than her uncle when he died. But she had been a heavy drinker for almost thirty years. In some ways, it's a wonder she didn't have problems sooner. Anyway, I've asked you here to let you know the contents of her will."

He opened the document in front of him and waited until he had Wil's attention. "A few years ago, as I think you know, she made over the stables, the Lodge, and some of the adjoining land to Felicity Evans. However the house and one hundred and forty acres are still part of her estate. This, and any money, both in the bank and invested, she left to you."

Wil gasped. She hadn't expected this. Kim had set up a trust fund for her, to be accessed when she turned twenty-five. But she hadn't expected Kim to die before she reached that age.

"There are just two other bequests; five hundred thousand pounds to Adriana McPherson, and twenty-five thousand pounds to a women's hostel in Nottingham. That last one surprised me. Perhaps it means something to you." Wil nodded, tears welling up. She knew only too well; it was the amount of money her mother had stolen from Kim, and Nottingham was the place where her body had been found. It was a message she thought sadly—a message of forgiveness.

"Oh, and she left this letter for you." He passed a large envelope across the desk to her. "That's another reason I think she planned it. She sent this to me a month ago with instructions to give it to you on the occasion of her death."

"When did she make the will?"

"Three years ago. I commended her at the time since so many people her age don't think of it and end up dying intestate. But she would have wanted to ensure none of her immediate family would benefit. From what she said at the time, she considered you to be her only family."

Wil did burst into tears then. The solicitor came around from behind his desk and held her gently.

"I should have been here for her. Why didn't she tell me she was ill? I wouldn't have gone away."

"You know what she was like. She wouldn't have thanked you for fussing around. In fact, it wouldn't surprise me if she encouraged you to go."

"You're right. I'd originally only planned on a few weeks. She said I should make it a few months. She knew how much I'd loved Italy. I had always wanted to go back and explore more of the country. Since I didn't take a gap year after my A-Levels, she said it was something I should do."

"Small comfort, I know, but at least you were doing what she wanted you to do."...

Wil came back to the present and gripped the now-cold mug of coffee in her hands. She had been aware of Ade's concern when Sally mentioned the last chapter she would need to conclude the biography. The envelope the solicitor had handed her contained a letter and a photograph. Wil still had both. Ade suggested, more than once, that she should burn the letter and scatter it along with Kim's ashes. But she had kept it, not wanting to relinquish her final precious connection with the writer. Wil could recall the day she finally found the courage to read it, and the words were imprinted indelibly on her mind.

...With trembling hands, she opened the envelope; it was only a single sheet and, unusual for Kim, not typed. The handwriting was ungainly, as it would be with someone unaccustomed to using a pen. It was like a first draft with words crossed out, other words added, and in some places, splodges of what could have been tears but were more likely whisky. The grammar wasn't up to Kim's usual standard either, but the tone of voice was all hers.

*Dear Wil,*

*If you're reading this, I guess it's happened. I'm dead. I'm sorry I won't see you grow older. I wish I could have been the person you wanted me to be. I'm glad Ade's been there for you when I wasn't. I hope you can forgive me. I always meant to try harder, but never really managed it.*

*I screwed up with Grace as well. I'm not proud of that either. But the big screw up was with your mother. It's taken a long time but I have finally pieced together what happened in those last days with me and Ginny.*

*I was very much in love with your mother. It still hurts when I think of the way she died. There are so many things I did wrong that I can't really point to anything that would have changed the way things happened.*

*Firstly, I fell in love with her. Why was that wrong? Because she didn't love me. And I didn't know that until it was too late.*

*I gave her the money. I know I let everyone think she stole it. She didn't. It was a present. What I couldn't face admitting until now—I was trying to buy her love. She said she needed the money to cover a debt. It had to be cash. I didn't ask the right questions.*

*Her temper, well I guess you know all about what she was capable of. On that night when it all went so wrong I told her she could have the money but I wanted her to agree to stay with me. I think I had sensed she was leaving me. She totally lost it. Apart from ripping into the furniture and throwing things around, she hit me. When I was in hospital, the doctors thought the broken ribs and two black eyes were from the car crash. They weren't. They were from her berserk attack. I couldn't fight back. I just wanted her to want to be with me.*

*The problem is it didn't end with her death. I never stopped loving her. I managed to block out those final hours so successfully for so long because I didn't want to believe it.*

*I know you blamed yourself for what happened. Maybe we would never have met if you hadn't turned up when you did. But it wasn't your fault.*

*It wasn't your fault I fell in love with the wrong person. I write fiction. I should know these things. Every great plot device revolves around love and betrayal. Shakespeare had it so right with that line from Romeo and Juliet: "These violent delights have violent ends..."*

*It wasn't your fault I couldn't see through her lies and deceptions. It wasn't your fault that I wouldn't listen to well-meaning friends who tried to warn me off.*

*Winterbourne has always been a special place for me. I think it is for you too. That's why I want you to have it. If you don't want it, then do with it what you wish. But I would like to think you will keep it for me.*

*With all the love (that I never gave you),*
*Kim.*

*P.S. This is a picture I've always treasured.*

*P.P.S. Say, 'Hey' to Ade...the best friend I could ever wish for.*

*P.P.P.S. Did I say I'm sorry? Please be happy.*

Wil shook the envelope and the photograph fell out. She recognised it at once. It was the two of them caught in the act of throwing snowballs at each other, both grinning madly. Grace must have taken it, that snowy Christmas long ago, back in Narnia.

She started to shake uncontrollably. She wanted so much to talk to Kim. Why had she left her? It was so needless. If only she could have talked to Wil like this when she was alive...

That question had tortured Wil for years. But the comfort was in knowing that she had fulfilled the writer's dying wish. She had kept Winterbourne for her. And now that she and Gaby were starting a family there was the hope that this special place would be kept for generations to come. And above all, she owed it to Kim's memory to be happy.

The buzzing from the house intercom caught her attention. Wil picked up the receiver. Rita's voice came through speaking quickly. It took Wil a moment to catch up with the words she thought she'd heard. "Gaby's gone into labour."

Rita met her as she reached the hall. "Don't worry, I've called Emma and she's on her way but Gaby wants you. She's in the study. I wanted her to go up to your room but she insisted on staying in there. I'm just going to get some towels and hot water."

When they had discussed the option of a home birth, Gaby had told her that the study was where she wanted to do it. Wil fought back the rising panic, took a deep breath and opened the door.

†

Ade had helped Rita carry water into the study, but once Emma arrived, the room felt too crowded with Teresa now there as well. She offered to let the guests know what was happening and that it was likely that the evening meal would be delayed.

Ade phoned Mark to let him know the birth was imminent, but he said they were really busy in the pub and he wouldn't be able to leave just yet. With everything thawing, the villagers were out in force. She thought that he probably wasn't too keen on seeing the business end of things, and she couldn't blame him. She didn't want to watch either.

JJ was the only one of the guests in the lounge when she checked.

"Hi, have you seen any of the others recently?"

"Candice and Mags were in the pool, but that was a while ago. Don't know about the other two."

*Not hard to guess what they were up to*, Ade thought. "Right. I'll put notes under their doors. The baby's due to make an appearance this evening, so our dinner plans are a bit up in the air right now. I'll keep you posted. Will you be staying in here?"

"Yeah. I want to finish this." JJ held up the book she was reading. "It's really good. Are her books still in print?"

"Yes. All the Amy Ransom ones anyway. Print and eBook."

"Great. I've never had much time for reading, but I could really get into these."

Ade smiled at JJ and left her to it. She went upstairs to print out a notice to put under the guest doors. And a sign to put on the study door: Birth in Progress. Do Not Disturb.

She only hoped for all their sakes, but most of all for Gaby, that it wasn't going to be a lengthy process.

After she distributed the notices and the sign, she went into the kitchen. Rita had done the lunch clean up so everything was tidy, just one half-drunk mug of coffee on the table. Checking the holiday menu on the wall, she found canapés and pre-dinner drinks were scheduled for six-thirty, an hour off.

Cooking wasn't her department but she knew where to look for information. Gaby was incredibly well organised and Ade easily located the Christmas file, a binder with all the meal plans and recipes printed out.

Smoked salmon and cream cheese blinis looked a bit complicated. Ade wondered if carrot sticks and mayo would suffice. Luckily she was saved from having to make a decision with the arrival of Rose and Felicity.

Rose peered over her shoulder to look at the menu and laughed. "So, Ade. Would you like to get started on the blini mix?"

Ade handed her the binder and backed away. "All yours now. I'll do the drinks."

"How's it going?" Felicity asked, going to the sink to wash her hands. "Rita said the contractions were ten minutes apart when she rang."

"I've no idea what that means. Where's Guido?"

"Doing a man thing."

"Meaning?"

"He's gone to the pub."

"That makes sense. Maybe we should skip this part of the programme and just all go to the pub."

"What is it about living that you don't like?" Felicity countered.

Ade nodded. She didn't want to raise the wrath of Rita, never mind Gaby, if she failed to ensure the smooth running of the operation whilst those two were otherwise engaged.

"Okay. So what do you need me to do first?"

†

Guido glanced around the pub as he entered. All the tables were taken but there was a space left at the bar. He seated himself on the stool and waited for Mark to notice him.

"*Prego*. Pint of Sheep Shit," he said when the landlord came over.

"You'll get it poured over you if you keep calling it that," Mark said as he pulled a glass from the shelf above his head.

"Ah. You wet baby's head, not mine."

"How's it going?"

"No idea. I stay out of way."

"Good plan. I'm with you, mate." Mark placed the drink in front of him. "On the house, Grandad."

Guido raised his beer glass. "*Nonno*."

"*Nonno*?" Mark looked puzzled. "Is that an Italian toast?"

"No. *Nonno* is grandad. My wife, she is *nonna*."

"Okay. *Nonno* it is, then." Mark smiled at him before moving away to serve another customer.

Guido sipped his beer, listening to the sounds of talk and laughter as people enjoyed each other's company in the pleasant surroundings. He liked English pubs, especially country ones like this that still had the old style. It was like walking into someone's home. He had to admit it was one thing the English did well. That and the beer.

Mark returned to his end of the bar and leaned over to ask, "Do you think it will be long?"

"I'm no..." Guido searched for the word, "...expert. But Teresa say maybe minutes, maybe hours."

"Jesus!"

"He no help." Guido reached over and patted his arm. "Nothing you can do. Just wait. They phone when baby comes."

Mark nodded and started pulling another pint.

Guido gave him what he hoped was a sympathetic smile. Babies came out when they were ready. Gabriella was a healthy young woman and she was in good hands with the midwife. All his children and other grandchildren had been born at home with no complications. Everything would be fine. He drained his glass and gratefully accepted the full one Mark placed in front of him.

# Chapter Eight

## Departures

Wil gazed down at the tiny form nuzzling Gaby's breast. Mother and child looked content. She reached out and touched the baby's hand. A small finger connected with hers.

"She's so beautiful," Wil whispered. "Like her mother." Placing light kisses on both their foreheads she moved reluctantly off the bed. "I need to go and say goodbye to the guests. Are you sure you don't mind me asking Clare to stay?"

Gaby smiled up at her. "Not at all, *cara*."

"Okay. I'll be back as soon as I can."

"No rush. We'll both be going to sleep when she's finished feeding."

Wil closed the bedroom door gently and made her way downstairs with newfound buoyancy in her step. The birth had gone smoothly with no complications. Holding Gaby's hand throughout, she had feared for her, seeing the pain etched on her face during each contraction. But when Emma came, she assured Wil everything was fine, and the baby obligingly made her appearance only an hour after the midwife's arrival.

Seeing the look of pure joy on Gaby's face as she held the baby for the first time was something she would always treasure. When she held little Heather Teresa in her own arms and looked into the almost black eyes, she knew the waiting and wondering had all been worth it.

Mark and Guido turned up not long after and were both immediately entranced by the child. Wil's worries about parenting faded away as she realised how lucky they were. This baby had everything she had lacked. A proper family.

†

The decision to stay at Winterbourne until after the New Year was an easy one. Clare had no definite plans and when Wil extended the invitation to Sally as well, it was a "no brainer."

Sally was emerging from the bathroom, hair wet from her shower, as Clare returned to the room invigorated by her swim and her conversation with Wil. Clare covered the distance between them in three strides.

"How do you feel about staying here for a bit longer?" she asked, grinning down at the smaller woman.

"I was planning to check into the B&B in the village."

"No need. Wil's invited both of us to stay. They don't have any new guests until the end of January. Not that I can stay that long. I have to be in London next week anyway."

Sally pulled her towel tighter around her body. "That's fantastic."

"And she says she's ready to talk to you whenever you want."

"Are you sure I'm not dreaming this?" Sally walked over to the window seat and sat down. "What's changed?

Clare looked over her head, seeing the lawn outside. Two big lumps of snow were all that was left of the snow horse. The metal sculpture horses continued their grazing unperturbed.

"The birth, I guess. A reminder of life beginning, not ending. Time to look forward, rather than back."

Sally patted the seat next to her. "That's far too deep a thought for this time of the morning. Come here and give me a kiss."

As soon as their lips met and Clare felt her body responding to the feel of soft breasts pressed against her, both their stomachs rumbled loudly. They pulled apart, laughing.

"Time for breakfast, I think." Sally gave her a playful push. "You need to keep your strength up. I have plans for you."

†

Ade hugged JJ as they waited in the hallway for Candice and Mags to come down from their room.

"Thanks for the loan of the sports bag. I'll get it back to you," JJ said when Ade released her.

"No need. I've got three more just like it at home." Ade smiled at her. "I know you won't have the best of memories, but I do hope you'll come back sometime."

"Actually, I have some pretty good memories. Maybe Shelley did me a favour. The last two days have given me a different perspective. I know it won't be easy when I get home and there are reminders of her everywhere, but I know I can deal with it."

The other two arrived at the bottom of the stairs. Mags smiled and nodded to them before carrying on outside with the suitcases. Candice stopped and tapped Ade on the arm.

"I've been thinking about your Wi-Fi situation. You could build your own mast. I know I read somewhere about someone who did that and it worked really well."

"Thanks. I had thought about it myself, but in the end we decided that there were benefits to not having a reliable connection."

"How's that?"

"Well, look what happened this week. You guys actually had to talk to each other. We figure we're doing people a favour when they get a bit of a break from relying on their devices for entertainment."

Candice laughed. "Right. I guess you'll be adding group skinny-dips to your programme then."

They were all laughing when Mags came back in. "What's so funny?"

"We were just recalling our Christmas swim," JJ told her.

"Oh, yeah!" Mags put her arm around Candice's shoulders. "That was amazing!"

Ade looked from one to the other. "We aim to please. Anyway, as I said to JJ, we hope you all will come again. I know it's a long way for you two, but if you are ever in the country again, please look us up."

"We certainly will," Candice said. "And we'll tell all our friends."

"That's what we like to hear." Wil joined them.

They all turned to look at her.

"Congratulations!" Candice was the first to react.

"Thanks, but I don't feel like I did much."

"How's the new mum and the baby? Did you get any sleep?"

Ade smiled to herself. Candice was on good form.

"On and off. Guess we'll get used to it. Anyway, I just wanted to say goodbye. It's been a bit different this year with the snow and everything."

"No need to apologise. It's been great." Mags surprised Ade by moving in for a hug.

Candice hugged Wil as well and said, "I guess we better head off. We've got a long drive."

"You're not going anywhere until we've had hugs too." Clare's voice carried down the long hallway from the kitchen.

After more hugs all around, the group moved outside. Mags held the passenger door open for Candice before moving to the driver's side of the car. JJ climbed into the back seat. They all waved until the car had disappeared around the first bend in the drive.

"That went well," Ade commented drily. "Better put in an order for snow next Christmas."

# Epilogue

## Ceremonies

"I've never seen this place in summer. It's gorgeous." Clare gazed around at the abundance of greenery enhanced by the colours of the flowers in carefully tended flowerbeds. They were standing on the patio at the back of the house where other guests were gathering.

"Guess that's why they chose September for the wedding," Sally replied. "In another month or two, it will look more like it did at Christmas."

"And having a wedding and a christening on the same day. Good planning."

Clare looked down at the woman next to her. They had come a long way since their Christmas liaison. She had gone back to Sydney for two months, getting in the last of the warm weather in Oz before coming back to start the filming schedule for the TV series. Sally joined her for three weeks in February but she had been anxious to return to London to continue work on the biography.

The last six months had been productive and happy times for both of them. The TV series was due to be screened in the run-up to Christmas, with the concluding part showing on Christmas Day. And Sally's book was in the final production stages. She had presented Wil with a proof copy when they arrived at Winterbourne House the day before.

"Hey, Clare!"

She turned to see a familiar figure approaching. "Hey, JJ. You scrub up well. Nice suit."

"You're not badly turned out yourself. Hi, Sally. Oh, and this is Kate."

Clare smiled at the woman whom she now noticed was holding JJ's hand, an attractive brunette whose summer dress showed off her attributes nicely. *An improvement on the last one, Surly Shelley*. That wasn't a thought she could utter aloud so she settled for, "Pleased to meet you, Kate."

"I've seen all your movies," Kate said shyly.

"Gosh. I haven't seen all of them myself."

"How's the filming going for the TV series?" JJ asked.

"Almost done. We've got the final few scenes for the last episode to do next week."

"Will you be going back home?"

Clare felt Sally stiffen beside her. This was a sore topic. She was committed to returning to Australia to fulfill another acting contract and had asked Sally to come with her. But the writer was having difficulty contemplating a move to the other side of the world. And she wasn't going to make a decision before the official launch of her book later that month. This was proving to be a real test of their relationship. Was it just an affair? Were they destined to go their separate ways? These were questions neither of them was willing to face head on just yet.

"Yes, I've got some work there." She was relieved that any further questioning was interrupted by Felicity Evans who was asking the guests to make their way to the ceremony site. The wedding invitations had suggested sensible footwear as the wedding was taking place in a clearing in the woods.

†

Ade counted the champagne glasses, looking up when Rita arrived in the kitchen.

"The christening went well. Teri didn't even cry."

The baby's full name was Heather Teresa Brunetti. But ever since her birth, everyone agreed Heather was too serious a name for the happy, smiling cherub. "She can choose when she's older," Wil said, but Ade was sure that the nickname would stick. Needless to say, *Nonna* Teresa was pleased.

The christening had taken place that morning in the local church. The vicar was happy to conduct the wedding ceremony in a woodland glade, but had insisted on doing the christening indoors.

"Teri hardly ever cries. Only when she's hungry. A bit like someone else I know." Rita grinned at her.

Ade ignored the dig. "How's Gaby doing?"

"She looks absolutely amazing in her dress but she worries that Wil won't like it."

"Honestly! The only thing Wil won't like is thinking how long it's going to take to get her out of it."

Rita shook her head. "I know. Anyway, best woman, I've been asked to check that you've got the rings."

233

"If you knew how many times I've been asked that today…"

†

Wil closed the book and gazed out across the lawn, not seeing anything. The biographer had done a fine job. Some of the photos she hadn't seen before. Clare had contributed stunning ones from the times she had spent with Kim in Sydney and San Francisco. Thelma Barton, surprisingly, had previously unpublished photos from literary events Kim had attended—readings and book signings.

She looked down at the cover. Kim's face smiled up at her. She could almost see the twinkle in her eyes, that moment when she was about to annihilate her in a Scrabble game by putting down a seven-letter word using the 'Q' covering a triple-letter square.

Focusing on the scene outside the window, Wil watched as Clare and Sally were joined by JJ and a woman she didn't know. Their conversation was interrupted by Felicity, doing her job as head usher. They had asked if she and Rose wanted to make it a double wedding. Felicity had given her a gruff no and muttered something about it being a ridiculous notion at their age. Rose just smiled sweetly and said they didn't want to intrude on their special day.

Guido came into view as the last of the guests disappeared. He gestured, indicating that she needed to come out now.

Time for her to make a move. She put the book on the table and stood. She silently said goodbye to Kim and thanked her for all that she had given her. But now it was time to move on with the next chapter in her own life.

A chapter filled with more laughter than tears. Gaby was already talking about wanting to have another child.

Wil walked out into the sunshine, anticipating the moment when she would put a wedding ring on the finger of the woman she loved.

## About the Author

## Jen Silver

Jen lives near Hebden Bridge in West Yorkshire with her long-term partner whom she married in December 2014. She has always enjoyed reading an eclectic range of genres including sci-fi, fantasy, historical fiction, and lesbian fiction. As well as reading and writing, her other activities include golf and archery. Her firsthand experience of an archaeological dig and a lifelong interest in Roman history were the creative forces behind her first published novel, *Starting Over,* released by Affinity in October 2014. The second book in the series, *Arc Over Time*, was published in May 2015 and the third book, *Carved in Stone*, in February 2016. Jen insists that she didn't set out to write a trilogy, but the characters demanded a proper conclusion to the story. A stand-alone romance, *The Circle Dance* was published in March 2016.

Contact Jen at jenjsilver@yahoo.co.uk, friend her on Facebook, or visit her blog: https://jenjsilver.wordpress.com.

# Other Books from Affinity eBook Press

The Review by Annette Mori
Silver Lining, a successful lesbian romance writer, is just starting to come out of the dark tunnel after her wife's untimely death. She has a crazy idea to sponsor a contest where the first reader who posts a review wins a home cooked meal. Who will come out the winner, the past, the present, or the unknown stalker?

South of Heaven by Ali Spooner
Kendra Drake thinks her life is complete. She has taken over as Captain of her father's shrimp boat. As a favor to her father, Kendra has agreed to give fellow shrimper Lindsey Bowen a chance to work on the boat. Kendra is fighting against mother nature, the open waters, and herself. Still, Lindsey finds a way into Kendra's heart. Will it only last for the summer?

Catch to Release by Lacey Schmidt
On the verge of finally releasing her own record label, lesbian folk-rock star, Shay Greenaura, finds herself caught up in more than just her music. Addison Weller, a former Diplomatic Security Services agent is called in to assess the threats against Shay. Follow this fast-paced adventure to its surprising romantic conclusion.

Ready for Love by Erin O'Reilly
Kylie Wilcox's life dramatically changed with the death of

her husband. Dr. LJ Evans, a renowned archaeologist, needed and wanted nothing but her work for her happiness. Their worlds are about to collide and lives will be altered forever.

Neptune's Ring by Ali Spooner
In the sequel to *Venus Rising*, Nat and Liz, owners of Venus Rising, invite Levi and Vanessa to join them in a venture for a new club on another island. They find the perfect place in an unfinished resort, Neptune's Ring. While on the island, Levi is drawn into a mystery involving secret compartments and a murder. Join the characters in this page-turning adventure, filled with steamy romance, intrigue, and an unsolved murder.

The Ultimate Betrayal by Annette Mori
Lara is a successful, beautiful, charming financier. She is also a total control freak, so whatever Lara wants, Lara makes sure she gets. Rachel is Lara's fun-loving, charming, irresistible wife. Sophia's surprise visit to see Lara sets in motion a number of life-changing events for them all. Hell has no fury like a woman scorned.

Keeping Faith by TJ Vertigo
Join the antics of Reece, Faith, Cori, Vi, and even The Animal, one last time in *Keeping Faith*. Faith has finally made the big screen, but how will Reece handle her success? Will the love that they share be enough to save their relationship and soothe The Animal?

Bound by Ali Spooner
A rogue master vampire threatens the existence of the New Orleans vampire clan. Lord Jordan enlists Devin Benoit,

sister of the Baton Rouge Alpha, and her witch lover, Tia, to assist with cleansing the city from potential disaster.

The Circle Dance by Jen Silver
Jamie Steele has moved to another town, trying to forget the heartbreak of losing her lover of six years. Sasha Fairfield finds her thoughts taken up with her ex-lover and thinks she wants Jamie back. Follow this captivating romance as love dances through the lives of these women to its surprising conclusion.

Search for the White Moon by Natalie London
Kathryn Austin, a government agent, is given opera singer, Adriana Desi, as her new assignment. Their lives and futures are in danger as the White Moon terrorists hunt them. Immerse yourself in this fast-paced romantic thriller by debut author Natalie London.

Take Me as I Am by JM Dragon & Erin O'Reilly
When Jo Lackerly and Thea Danvers meet, an unexpected friendship develops, proving a catalyst for both women to change their lives irrevocably. Follow them on a journey of discovery that will have your heart smiling, blood boiling, and senses entangled in a wonderful romance.

Carved in Stone by Jen Silver
Join the characters from *Starting Over* and *Arc Over Time* in this final book from the Starling Hill trilogy. Ellie Winters thinks she might be going mad when the ancient queen wants a proper burial for herself and her consort. *Carved in Stone* has romance, adventure, a treasure hunt, and happy endings for all, living and dead.

Anywhere, Everywhere by Renee MacKenzie
Gwen Martin's life in the Ten Thousand Islands area changes irrevocably when Piper Jackson comes into her life. Without trust, can the budding relationship between Gwen and Piper survive? Or will the answers to the questions continue to haunt them?

Venus Rising by Ali Spooner
Levi Johnson arrives at Venus Rising, an exclusive lesbian-only tropical resort in the Virgin Islands and finds more than she expected—a sizzling-hot love triangle. Torn between her attraction to two women, she struggles to choose the right woman to share her life.

The Devil's Tree by Ali Spooner
Torn between her love for the pack and her need to find what's missing in her life, Devin Benoit travels to New Orleans. Will the previous happenings at the Devil's Tree help or hinder Devin in the fight of her life, and the life of Tia, the woman who now owns her heart?

The Beggars' Coppice by Erica Lawson
Edda Case is a woman in crisis who discovers that things are not as they seem. Is it truly a message for her from beyond the grave or is something more sinister taking place? Can Edda solve the mystery of *The Beggars' Coppice*?

Locked Inside by Annette Mori
How much does the power of love matter to someone who must overcome obstacles far greater than most people face in a lifetime?

Line of Sight by Ali Spooner
Sasha and her lover Kara are back. Continue the thrilling adventures of this couple from the Sasha Thibodaux series.

Requiem for Vukovar by Angela Koenig
*Requiem for Vukovar* continues the Refraction series and the exploits of Jeri O'Donnell and her partner, Kelly Corcoran. In an epic siege largely ignored by the wider world, Kelly, who was prepared to give up comforts and certainties when she became part of Jeri's nomadic life, encounters more than physical danger. Her ability to maintain her core integrity is assaulted by the inevitable ugliness of war. For Jeri, the true battle is confronting her attraction to violence as she struggles against losing herself in the exhilaration of combat.

Against All Odds by JM Dragon
From award-winning and bestselling author JM Dragon, with significant updates by Erin O'Reilly, comes an original tale of romance where everything seems to be stacked against two women whose destinies bring them together. Life however takes a twisted path, setting both Steph and Louise in directions they never thought possible. Will love win out against all odds, or will love be forever lost?

The Settlement by Ali Spooner
The outpouring of love and friendship toward Cadin helps her on her path to healing and learning to trust her heart to love once again. Join bestselling author Ali Spooner on this sensational journey that ends with a heartwarming romance.

E-Books, Print, Free e-books

Visit our website for more publications available online.

www.affinityebooks.com

Published by Affinity E-Book Press NZ LTD
Canterbury, New Zealand

Registered Company 2517228

36490932R00140

Printed in Great Britain
by Amazon